JENNINGS AT LARGE

More Jennings books to watch out for:

and the brand-new Jennings book
JENNINGS AGAIN!

Author's note

Each of the Jennings books is a story complete in itself.
Apart from the first title, JENNINGS GOES TO
SCHOOL, the books can be read in any order, and for
this reason I have chosen some of the later titles for
early publication in this edition.

Anthony Buckeridge

JENNINGS
AT
LARGE

Anthony Buckeridge

MACMILLAN
CHILDREN'S BOOKS

NICOLA SUZANNE
her book

Copyright © Anthony Buckeridge 1977, 1992
Illustrations © Macmillan Publishers Ltd 1992

First published 1977 by William Collins & Sons Co Ltd

Paperback edition with illustrations by Rodney Sutton,
published 1992 by
MACMILLAN CHILDREN'S BOOKS
A division of Pan Macmillan Children's Books Limited
London and Basingstoke
Associated companies throughout the world

ISBN 0–333–574079

A CIP catalogue record for this book is available from
the British Library

Phototypeset by Intype, London

Printed in Great Britain by Richard Clay Ltd, Bungay, Suffolk

CONTENTS

LIST OF
ILLUSTRATIONS

Chapter 1

Crossing off the Days

The boy in the end bed sat propped against his pillow, speaking into a tooth-mug held before his lips like a microphone.

"Hullo, Earth! . . . Hullo, Earth! . . . Moon calling Earth! This is Space-Pilot Jennings calling Mission Control. Are you receiving me?"

From the bed across the gangway a fair-haired boy in glasses and blue-striped pyjamas removed a similar tooth-mug from his left ear and called back, "Can't hear a thing, Jen. Take your face out of your beaker and stop mumbling."

The astronaut jammed his jaw into the tooth-mug and waggled his chin experimentally. To his delight the beaker stayed in place, moving up and down with his chin like a plastic beard. There was no point in old Darbi telling him to speak up, he thought: with so much noise going on in the dormitory it was no wonder that messages from the Moon were failing to get through. He removed his chin-beard and shouted above the clamour of boys' voices about him, "OK, I'll start again. If you can't hear, try lip-reading?"

"Can't you get through, Jennings?" Venables, an untidy eleven-year-old in the next bed, hooted with derision. "What's the dialling code to ring up the Earth from the Moon?" he demanded. "If I were you I'd reverse the charges. It's a long-distance call, don't forget!"

Jennings ignored the advice. "Moon calling Earth! . . . Moon calling Earth!" he bellowed into his plastic mug. "We landed here at tea-time and have been doing – er – er . . ." (What *had* they been doing? . . . Oh yes!) "We have been doing a lot of dangerous exploits. No sign of any planet-dwellers around these parts. Just a lot of old stars and stripes and hammers and sickles lying about."

The man at Mission Control. (*alias* C. E. J. Darbishire) tossed his makeshift earphone aside. He'd had enough of this game to be going on with and, in any case, he wanted to finish his library book before the duty master came in to call silence.

But Venables decided the make-believe was worth carrying a stage further. No sign of any planet-dwellers! He'd soon put that right!

Flinging back the bedclothes, he jumped up and stood bouncing on his bed like a clown on a trampoline. "Moonman hide in crater when Earthman touch down," he announced in the metallic tones of a television robot. "Moonman exterminate Earthman! Big Chief Moonshine make Earthman bite pumice dust."

He signalled for support to Temple and Atkinson, further down the dormitory, who at once stood up on their beds chanting aggressive slogans at the tops of their penetrating voices.

"Earthman, go home! . . . Earthman, go home! . . . Earthman, out, out, out!"

The noise was deafening – until the dormitory door swung open and Mr Carter stood on the threshold, his fingers in his ears and his eyes closed in mock anguish.

The shouting died and the demonstrators got back into bed, safe in the knowledge that on this night of all nights, the duty master was unlikely to say very much about the noise unless it threatened to get out of hand . . . On any other night, *yes*: but not tonight, for this was the last night of term.

The last night of term is different from all those that have gone before; it is a time when excitement bubbles up in anticipation of tomorrow's freedom; a time when school rules can be relaxed to stop the pressure from building up into an explosion.

Mr Carter, the senior master at Linbury Court School, had been teaching boys long enough to have gained a deep insight into the workings of the youthful mind. The boys liked him and he enjoyed their confidence; so even at this time of unaccustomed freedom they had no thought of taking advantage of him.

The duty master unplugged his ears. "Tomorrow will come when it's ready," he said. "No amount of shouting will make it arrive sooner, so for the sake of all our eardrums I suggest we cut the volume down to a mere ninety-five decibels, or so."

"Sorry, sir, but we had to speak loudly," Venables

3

explained. "You see, the planet-dwellers were ganging up on the Earthmen and— "

"And I was trying to broadcast my famous first words to the human race," the astronaut broke in. "Only I couldn't get through because Mission Control wanted to finish his library book before you called silence, sir."

Mr Carter had no intention of calling for immediate silence in an atmosphere so charged with excitement. He was willing to wait until the taut guy ropes of their restlessness had slackened of their own accord. In half an hour they would be ready to settle down for the night: but first they must be allowed to greet the end of term with the song made up by past generations of Linburians and added to, over the years, by anyone able to express an apt comment in verse.

By tradition, the song was sung in the dormitories every night during the final week of term, building up into an ear-splitting climax on the last evening of all.

"If the Moonmen will call off their demo they'll just have time for a farewell performance of *Crossing off the Days*," Mr Carter announced. "But they'd better get a move on because I'm aiming to call silence in here before my supper gets cold."

Dormitory Four needed no urging. Sitting bolt upright in their beds, they awaited the signal from Jennings who now stood on his pillow holding his tooth-brush like a conductor's baton. Darbishire produced his recorder from his locker and sat poised to accompany the choir (omitting those quavers that were always too fast for him to keep up with).

"Fire away!" said Mr Carter, turning to leave the

room. "See if you can get through it in four minutes flat."

As he went downstairs to see what was happening in Dormitory Two, the strains of the Linbury end-of-term song pursued him all the way down to the next landing.

"The term is nearly over, we've been crossing off
    the days
Until tomorrow morning when we go our different
    ways.
Seven days, six days, five days, four days, three
    days, two days, *One*!
And the holidays will really have begun."

The tune was lively, the tempo fast. Nobody could remember who had composed it, for it was a hotch-potch of improvisations borrowed from older melodies. Then came the chorus in a different rhythm; and taken up now by the dormitories on the lower landing in unison with the boys on the floor above. Passing the open door of Dormitory Three, Mr Carter winced as the chorus assailed his ears at full volume.

"Excuse our breaking out in song
Believe you me, it won't last long.
We'll let off steam and then we'll stop,
Either that or we'll blow our top.

"For the end of term is drawing near,
Holidays will soon be here.

Pack our bags and we'll be off.
Linbury – goodbye!"

By now all the dormitories had joined in. The words of verse two, amplified by the well of the staircase, were wafted into the staffroom on the ground floor where Mr Wilkins was finishing off Form Three's reports.

"No more French and Latin, no more English, no more Maths.
No more risk of masters turning into psychopaths.
No examinations to confuse my poor old brain.
No more risk of going crazy with the strain."

Mr Wilkins paused in the act of writing his comments on Jennings' progress in mathematics. Judging by the boy's examination results there was little fear of *his* brain becoming unhinged by the strain of the term's work.

Upstairs in the dispensary, Matron was tidying shelves and putting away the medical equipment she would not be needing until the following term. The full-throated singing from Dormitory Six along the landing was loud enough to set the bottles rattling on the dispensary shelves.

"Goodbye lumpy mattress in my freezing dormit'ry.
Goodbye my school dinner and goodbye to my school tea;

Bullet-proof potatoes and bomb-proof hard-boiled
  eggs.
And goodbye to cocoa made from diesel dregs."

The song was sheer nonsense, of course, but Matron
couldn't help smiling at the parody of boarding school
life implied by the words . . . Freezing dormitory,
indeed, with the warm July sun still slanting in through
the western windows! They'd been keen enough on
their bomb-proof eggs at tea-time; and at supper they'd
queued up for second helpings of the cocoa they pro-
fessed to despise.

The flippant words and the catchy tune followed Mr
Carter along the corridor as he made his tour of the
dormitories. By the time he got back to the top landing
again the singers had reached the last verse.

"Hurry up, tomorrow, for tomorrow I shall be
  Miles away from boarding school, miles from
    Linbury.
  Seven weeks of liberty when we're let off the
    chain.
  Then it's back to the treadmill once again."

A final rousing chorus and the singers were ready to
settle down for the night, exhausted by their vocal
efforts. Indeed, when Mr Carter looked into Dormitory
Four to call silence, the only boy with enough breath
left for coherent speech was the astronaut in the end
bed who had resumed his news-bulletin from Outer
Space and was again trying to contact Mission Control.

7

"Stand by for important announcement! I'm going to repeat my famous first words in case you hadn't tuned in properly," he was saying into his plastic toothmug. "When I first stepped out on to the Moon I said to myself, 'Aha!' I said. 'It's just one small step for little old me, but a giant leap for mankind.' Make sure you copy it down right, because it'll go down in the history books."

But nobody was listening. Least of all Mission Control who was lying back on his pillow thinking of all the things he was hoping to do in the summer holidays. Darbishire's day-dreams seldom bore much resemblance to what actually happened in real life. But that didn't matter. On the last night of term there was ample excuse for any eleven-year-old to build up fantastic pictures in his mind.

At the end of every summer term Mr Carter would take a party of boys on a short holiday expedition. Sometimes they would go walking or rock-climbing in the Lake District; on other occasions they would spend a week in France or exploring the canals of the English Midlands. These expeditions were extremely popular and the boys considered it well worth while forfeiting a week of their summer holidays in order to take part. There was always keen competition to secure a place in the party and, as numbers were limited, Mr Carter made a point of choosing boys of roughly the same age and with similar interests when he compiled his list.

This year, for the first time, he had extended his invitation to Form Three and had arranged to take

8

eight of them for a short camping holiday on a farm in Surrey. It was his practice to include at least one other member of the staff to help him, and on this occasion Mr Wilkins had, with some misgiving, agreed to join the party.

Unlike Mr Carter, who remained calm in the face of chaos, Mr Wilkins became exasperated whenever some crisis arose which threatened to disrupt the smooth working of school routine. He was a large, burly man, with a powerful voice and a limited supply of patience; and though fond of the boys in his charge, he could never quite understand the way in which their minds appeared to work. To his way of thinking, the things boys said and the things boys did seemed utterly lacking in reason.

So, on the following morning while the rest of the school were departing by car or train to start their summer holidays, Mr Wilkins stood on the playground supervising the packing of the camping equipment into the school mini-bus.

"Come along now, you boys, don't waste time," he boomed at Temple, Atkinson and Bromwich who were struggling across the tarmac with a tent. "Bring that over to me: it'll go on the roof-rack."

Behind them came Venables carrying a wooden cage in which two mouse-like creatures were frisking about. Mr Wilkins stared at them in horror. "What on earth have you got there, Venables? Take them away at once!"

"Oh, but, sir, they've got to come with me. They're my pet gerbils and—"

"I don't care if they're your pet crocodiles. You're not taking them camping and don't you think it."

"But I *must*, sir," Venables protested. "I've got to take them home with me after camp. I couldn't put them in my trunk because they'd suffocate and there's nobody left at school to look after them."

"All right, all right." Despite his exasperation, Mr Wilkins had to admit that, in the circumstances, there was no alternative but to allow the boy to bring his wretched pets with him. Grudgingly, he found a space to stow the cage under one of the seats. But when, two minutes later, Martin-Jones arrived with a cello Mr Wilkins felt it was time to make a stand on the question of what sort of articles were suitable for a holiday under canvas.

"You silly little boy, you can't play an instrument that size in a small tent," he said. "Quite apart from the fact that there's no room, some clumsy little boy would be bound to put his foot through it if it's left lying about."

"But, sir, Mr Hind said I'd got to practise every day during the holidays because I've got my exam next term and—"

"You heard what I said, boy! If you want to play musical instruments in camp you'll have to settle for something no bigger than a mouth-organ."

Mr Wilkins had been doubtful about accepting the invitation to help at the summer camp. He had pointed out that he saw quite enough of the boys during term time without being encumbered with them in the holidays as well. But Mr Carter had been so persuasive and had painted the prospects of a week under canvas in such glowing colours, that his colleague had not only agreed to come but, for the last few days, had actually been looking forward to the expedition. Now, however, as the boys continued to arrive with such a bewildering stock of possessions, he felt his old doubts returning.

Why, for instance, should Rumbelow want to bring his model railway when it was obvious that there would be no electricity to connect it to! Why had they got to be lumbered with Darbishire's bookshelf (made during carpentry classes) merely because he had forgotten to send it home with his trunk! And what on earth was the use of Jennings bringing a table-tennis set to a sloping, windswept field where there wouldn't be anything resembling a ping pong table on which they could play!

Firmly Mr Wilkins refused to accept these items of so-called camping equipment: and it was as well that he did so for, by the time that tents, bedding, cooking stove and all the other essentials were stowed in the mini-bus, there was barely room for the campers, let alone the grown-ups in charge.

Chapter 2

Stormy Weather

They set off at eleven o'clock with Mr Carter driving, the eight boys packed like sardines amongst the equipment and Mr Wilkins perched on a wobbling bundle of blankets in the gangway between the seats. Their destination was Southcombe, a village which, though less than thirty miles from London, had retained its rural character despite the network of new roads and industrial estates which were growing up around it.

Mr Carter knew the district well and had obtained permission to set up his camp on farmland a short distance from the village. The meadow he had chosen was well away from the road, and access was difficult in the mini-bus which had to wind up a bumpy track and cross a steeply-sloping field in order to reach the site.

It was early afternoon when the party arrived, having stopped for a picnic lunch on the way.

The boys were in excellent spirits: Mr Wilkins less so, for he had had an uncomfortable journey on his wobbling bundle of bedding which had collapsed whenever the vehicle had rounded a bend. This had thrown

the boys into convulsions of maniacal laughter: and
when they were not laughing at his plight or expressing
their deepest sympathy in voices choked with glee, they
spent the time in asking ridiculous riddles and telling
terrible jokes – all of which Mr Wilkins had heard thirty
years before.

So he was not sorry when at last the bus jolted its
way over the hillocks to its destination.

"May I help you do the cooking, sir?" Jennings
asked him as the boys unloaded the van. "I'm quite
good at it, really. I helped my mother make a cake last
holidays."

"Did you indeed! And was it edible?"

"Well, yes and no, sir. The trouble was I'd been
making some plaster-of-Paris chessmen on the kitchen
table before we started, and while my mother was
weighing out the flour—"

"Don't tell me: I can guess what happened."

"Ah, no, sir! You've got it the wrong way round,"
Jennings explained. "I didn't get the plaster mixed up
with the flour: I got some cake-mix in my chessmen
moulds by mistake; and by the time they'd gone hard
we didn't know whether to eat two of the pawns and
the white queen or to play chess with them."

Mr Wilkins said, "Don't waste time talking nonsense. I want to get the camp set up before the rain
comes."

All the morning dark rain clouds had blotted out the
sun and a fresh wind had been threatening to blow up
into a gale. By now most of the equipment had been
unloaded: two sleeping tents for the boys, another for

13

the masters and a large, all-purpose tent to serve as a canteen and kitchen had been unrolled ready for erection. Beside them stood the cooking stove, airbeds, blankets and sleeping bags and a carton of crockery and cutlery.

Mr Carter looked at the bedding with a frown. "Those blankets shouldn't have been taken out until the tents were up," he said. "Get them under cover, quickly. If I'm not mistaken we're in for some rough weather." He turned to his colleague. "I'll walk down to the village with a couple of boys and fetch the provisions. Will you see to the tents while we've gone?"

"Of course," Mr Wilkins assured him. "I'll have the big one up before anything gets wet, you see if I don't."

Mr Carter went off to the village with Martin-Jones and Rumbelow, leaving Mr Wilkins with a crew of six willing helpers bubbling over with enthusiasm for the task on hand.

No sooner had they started work than a violent squall blew up from the south-west. The wind whistled across the exposed hillside and driving rain whipped the faces of the willing crew.

"Everything under cover, quickly!" Mr Wilkins ordered and there was a scurry of activity to get the bedding and the spare clothing back into the van.

"Shall we stay in the bus till it stops, sir?" Darbishire asked when everything of consequence had been rescued from the rain.

Mr Wilkins considered. They were already so wet that it could do them no harm to get wetter. "We'll carry on and get the tents up," he decided. "We don't want Mr Carter coming back to find we've just been sitting about all afternoon."

They started work on the big tent, hampered not only by the driving rain, but even more by the strong wind which had now increased almost to gale force. With water dripping down the necks of their anoraks they unrolled the tent, but when they tried to set it upright on its poles the flapping wet canvas dancing in the wind was too much for them to control.

Mr Wilkins stationed a boy at each pole, but their strength was unequal to the task, for no sooner would one corner be secured than another would be swept out of the hands of the helpers and the whole canopy would billow up into the air, uprooting the poles and threatening to go sailing away in a hedge-high take-off.

In this alarming situation, Mr Wilkins was desperate to get some tent pegs into the ground to anchor the straining canvas.

"Hold on tight, all of you," he encouraged his crew in a voice that carried above the noise of the wind. "We'll have it up in no time, as soon as I find the bag with the pegs in."

The peg-bag had been thrown back into the van when the rain started and was discovered underneath a pile of rucksacks after ten minutes' search. Then, armed with peg and mallet, Mr Wilkins set to work.

At the first stroke the mallet snapped in two, leaving him with the useless shaft in his hand.

"Doh! This is infuriating," he stormed, blinking his eyes against the stream of rain-water running down his face. "One of you boys go and find me a large stone to knock the pegs in with."

Five boys rushed off to obey the command, leaving Darbishire to support the tent all by himself. For some seconds he stood hugging his pole like a shipwrecked mariner lashed to a mast while all about him the canvas tore at its moorings. Then the tent collapsed in a heap smothering him in its folds.

The rescue of Darbishire and the search for a make-shift mallet took some little while, but at last Mr Wilkins was ready for another attempt to get the pegs into the ground.

The flint boulder provided by Venables in place of the mallet was equal to its task, but this time the tent peg doubled up like a hairpin under the impact of the blow. Muttering with frustration Mr Wilkins found another peg, but to his dismay a gentler tap produced the same result and it soon became clear that the sub-soil under the turf consisted almost entirely of large flints with a mere smattering of soil between one piece of rock and the next.

The master spent the next twenty minutes in digging out flints with a bent-pronged kitchen fork which was the only tool he could lay his hands on at short notice. Even so, his troubles were not over for, when the flints had been prised out, the soil that remained was too loose to give his pegs any lasting support.

Slowly and clumsily the flapping wet canvas was coaxed into position: and though the poles were leaning inwards, the pegs and guy ropes seemed to hold out some promise of withstanding the strain.

"It doesn't look very pretty, but at least it's up," Mr Wilkins panted as he hammered in the last peg and stood up. "All right, you boys, you can let go of the poles now."

He spoke too soon. For the next moment there came a shrill cry of alarm from the far side of the tent.

"Sir, sir! Emergency, sir: my peg's come out," cried Jennings. So much was obvious from the sudden alarming tilt at the north-west corner, and Mr Wilkins shouted back, "Hold on to the rope, boy. Hold on to the rope!"

"I can't, sir. It's stronger than I am. It's pulling too hard."

"Find something to tie it on to, till I get round!"

Jennings glanced about him. The mini-bus was parked a few feet away, within range of his guy-rope. "Hey, Venables, come and hang on to my pole while I fix the rope," he shouted.

While Venables braced himself against the tottering support, Jennings extended the guy-rope to its full length and tied it round the rear bumper of the van with a neat clove-hitch.

"OK, it's all right, now, sir. Firm as a rock!" he called, delighted at his ready solution to the problem. He turned to Venables and grinned. "This corner is the only one now that isn't wobbling."

"Never mind about the corners wobbling. My *knees* are wobbling on both cylinders after all this carry-on. I just want to get out of this hurricane before I get blown inside-out."

At that moment Martin-Jones came struggling up

17

the hill, bent double against the wind. He panted to a halt beside Mr Wilkins and said, "Message from Mr Carter, sir. He's got all the provisions and stuff down at the village shop, but he wants to keep the food dry, so will you go and meet him in the van."

"Fair enough; I'll go right away." Mr Wilkins was only too willing for a change of occupation. "Get under cover, you boys, and try and dry off a bit while I go to the village," he boomed, striding round the tent towards the mini-bus.

The boys scurried in through the tent-flap as Mr Wilkins climbed into the driving-seat and started the engine. Accelerating, he let in the clutch and the van lurched forward as though partly restrained by some heavy object at the rear. Then, recovering and gathering momentum, the vehicle moved forward a few yards over the rough ground.

Cries of dismay and shouts of warning rang out from behind the bus.

Alarmed, Mr Wilkins glanced in the driving-mirror. To his horror and amazement, what looked like an enormous vampire bat with outstretched wings was hovering in space behind the van, while cowering on the ground was his team of campers, their hands over their heads to protect themselves from the free-swinging tent-poles dangling like legs from the four corners of the flying apparition above them.

Mr Wilkins was so startled that for one confused moment he shot his foot down on the accelerator instead of on the brake. As the van leapt forward, a strong gust of wind caught the canvas tethered to the

Cries of dismay and shouts of warning rang out from behind the bus

bumper and the tent soared up like a kite before collapsing on the ground in a heap.

Speechless with baffled fury, Mr Wilkins stopped the van and got out. Thanks to some wretched little boy's idiotic prank, the work of the last hour-and-a-half had been reduced to a flapping mound of canvas.

"Which of you boys tied a guy-rope to my bumper?" he demanded when the power of speech returned.

"I did, sir," Jennings replied, rising from the pile of bodies huddled on the ground for fear of flying tent poles.

"Doh! You silly little boy! Now see what you've done." The master pointed to the wreckage with a quivering forefinger. "What in the name of thunder did you want to do a stupid thing like that for?"

"You told me to, sir."

"Me!" Mr Wilkins was thunderstruck. "I never said anything of the sort."

"Yes, sir. I told you my peg had come out and you said I was to tie the rope on to anything I could find. So I did a clove-hitch round the bumper and—"

"Doh! Of all the crazy places to tie it!"

"It was only for the time being, sir; I didn't know you were going to drive off in the bus. If only you'd told me what you were—"

"All right, all right, all right," Mr Wilkins snapped, annoyed that he, too, was not entirely free from blame.

There was only one thing for it. They would have to start from scratch and do the work all over again. It was infuriating! It was exasperating! . . . It was that boy, Jennings, as usual!

"Come along, now, all of you. Straighten out the canvas and then go and stand by your corners," the master told his reluctant crew.

They were all on their feet now that the danger had passed, but the wind was still blowing strongly and they had little stomach for the job on hand.

"Oh, sir! Not again, sir. Not all over *again*," Venables protested. "I'm still worn out with putting it up the first time."

"It's all Jennings' fault," Temple claimed. "I reckon he ought to put it up by himself."

"Ah, but if Sir hadn't driven the van away—"

"All right then, let Jennings help Sir to put it up, while we take it easy for a bit."

The happy, carefree atmosphere which should always prevail when setting up camp was in danger of degenerating into pointless bickering, and Mr Wilkins felt that, despite his exasperation, he must do something to restore the morale of his crew.

"We'll all stop arguing about whose fault it was and get back to work," he told them. It meant, of course, that Mr Carter would have to wait for his transport, but he couldn't leave boys like Jennings to put the tent up without a responsible grown-up in charge. No doubt Carter would understand!

But it was doubtful whether Mr Carter *did* quite understand when he and Rumbelow arrived back from the village on foot, having grown tired of waiting for the transport that never arrived.

For by this time the wind had dropped, the rain had stopped and the camp site was bathed in late afternoon

21

sunshine. Unlike his drenched and windswept colleague, Mr Carter had sheltered in the village shop
while the storm was raging and now returned warm,
dry and comfortable to see what progress had been
made during his absence. He was surprised that so little
had been done.

"Well really, Wilkins, I was expecting to find everything set up and the kettle boiling for a cup of tea,"
he said in mock protest. "And here you are still struggling with the first tent."

The mild banter was lost on Mr Wilkins who said
tersely, "We had problems."

"H'm! Well, I don't want to sound fussy, but I must
point out that you've got the entrance pointing straight
into the prevailing wind. I think it would be better
to take the tent down and put it up facing the other
way."

Mr Wilkins stared at his colleague in horror. "Take
it *down*!" he echoed. "Put it up *again*! I'd rather erect
a block of flats with my own hands than repeat what
I've had to go through this afternoon." He waved his
arms in distracted circles and his voice grew shrill in
protest. "Do you realise I've been working in a Force
Nine gale with the rain coming down like a car-wash!
And as if that wasn't enough I've had silly little boys
wrecking my efforts with a—"

"Never mind, Wilkins, you've made quite a good
start," Mr Carter interposed tactfully. "I suggest you
go and make the tea while the boys and I turn the tent
round."

Which is what happened! For under Mr Carter's

expert guidance the big tent was up and ready for use while Mr Wilkins was still wondering where to get the water from to make the tea.

Chapter 3

Right of Way

There was more rain that evening, but it did nothing to dampen the spirits of the campers. The big tent was proof against the weather – except in those places where Darbishire had traced patterns with his fingers against the inside walls while they were wet. There were other minor mishaps: someone had left the matches outside in the rain; Temple's air-bed, tossed down without due care, was deflated by a jagged piece of flint and the puncture had to be repaired with chewing-gum.

Mr Wilkins, too, had a problem. He couldn't find a level piece of ground on which to set up the cooking-stove which rocked like a dinghy in a gale whenever he touched it. He tried wedging first one foot, then another; but even when all four feet were supported, the stove was still tilted at an angle and he had to hold the kettle steady until it came to the boil: and when he started cooking the sausages for supper, all the hot fat ran down to one side of the frying-pan, overflowed and caught fire. This, in turn, ignited a tea towel hanging above the stove. In frantic haste the volunteer cook

24

seized the flaming towel, hurled it outside the tent and beat out the flames with Rumbelow's trainer.

When the meal was served, half the sausages were charred to a cinder and the other half were pink and raw; but nobody seemed to mind, and nobody slept any the worse.

After breakfast next morning, Mr Carter said, "I want two volunteers for camp duties."

Eight hands shot up, though one or two faltered a little when it was explained that the chosen pair would be working under the direction of Mr Wilkins.

"Rumbelow and Bromwich for camp duties, and the rest of you can come exploring with me," Mr Carter decided. "We'll make it a nature trail along the ridge and down through the wood and see what we can find."

So off they went, clustered round Mr Carter and bubbling over with enthusiasm. But while, in theory, they were taking in their surroundings, their conversation soon lapsed into a non-stop prattle of idiotic jokes and outrageous puns. Quite soon, Mr Carter called a halt.

"The purpose of this expedition is to get to know the countryside," he told them. "If, on the other hand, our object had been to find out who could ask the most ridiculous riddle about elephants, we needn't have bothered to leave camp."

"Oh, but we *are* observing wildlife and stuff," Jennings assured him. "It's going in through our eyes all the time we're asking our riddles, sir."

"Is it, indeed!"

"Yes, sir. For instance, that squirrel we saw just now

25

reminded me of the one about the grey animal with four legs, a tail and a trunk. Everyone thinks the answer's an elephant of course, but it's really a mouse going to boarding-school by train. Really funny, don't you think, sir!"

"Hilarious!" Mr Carter agreed solemnly. "But for the moment we'll forget elephants and see what smaller creatures we can identify as we go along."

And the next creature they came across, though smaller than an elephant, was a great deal larger than any squirrel, rabbit or hedgehog which they had been expecting to find . . . It was a donkey, standing still in the middle of the path near the entrance to the wood.

Darbishire said, "I can identify *him*, all right." He jotted down the discovery in his note-book.

"But what's he doing here, all by himself?" Venables queried. "He ought to be in a field, not wandering about. He could find himself on the motorway if he's not careful."

Temple, who seldom travelled far without food, produced some crumbling biscuits from the lining of his anorak and approached the animal with hand outstretched.

"Watch it! He might take your fingers off; he's got teeth like tombstones," Atkinson warned him. "Hold your hand flat."

The warning proved unnecessary, for the donkey took the offering with the gentlest curl of its top lip, and when the last of the biscuits had gone it stretched its neck forward awaiting more.

"That's all; you've had the lot," Temple explained,

walking away. But the donkey was not to be fobbed off so easily and followed at his heels, nudging him between the shoulder blades with its nose.

"Hey, push off, go away, beat it!" Temple protested with the animal breathing hard into his left ear. His complaints were ignored and for a hundred yards or more the party walked on with Temple trying to dodge his follower and the rest of the boys falling about with laughter at his discomfiture.

Mr Carter said, "You started something with those biscuits. You won't get rid of him easily, now."

"What's going to happen if he won't go away? We can't take him back to camp with us," Darbishire said.

"Why not?" said Jennings. "He'll soon push off when he's sampled Mr Wilkins' cooking."

The problem of how to get rid of the donkey was solved as they rounded the next bend of the track through the wood. Coming up the path towards them with a purposeful tread was a tall, middle-aged woman with untidy grey hair and a windswept complexion. She was wearing wellingtons and jeans and carrying a noose of rope; and at the sight of the approaching campers she threw up her hands in triumph.

"Ah! So you've found Epaminondas for me," she greeted them in ringing tones. "Stupid animal, always getting lost. Hasn't got the sense he was born with."

She strode up to the donkey, removed its nuzzling nose from Temple's armpit and slipped the noose over its head. "You silly old ass!" she went on in kindly tones. "You'll be in trouble if you go on like this. Me, too, if you start straying on to the major's property."

27

"We couldn't think what he was doing up here, all by himself," Venables told her. "Has he come far?"

"Not more than half a mile this time. My fault, of course; the paddock fence is so dilapidated it wouldn't stop a Christmas pudding from getting out – let alone a four-footed animal." She looked inquiringly at Mr Carter. "Perhaps your boys would like to lead him home for me and meet the rest of the menagerie."

Menagerie! The boys exchanged glances. Did she own a private zoo, by any chance?

They watched with interest as the tall woman walked over to Mr Carter and introduced herself. The two adults chatted together for a few minutes, after which Mr Carter turned to the boys and said, "Mrs Hockin has invited us to go and have a look at her animals, and from what she tells me the visit should be well worth while."

The boys were only too eager to accept the invitation.

"Splendid! You can lead Epaminondas," said Mrs Hockin, handing the rope to Temple. Her glance ranged round the group and came to rest upon Darbishire. "And you can ride him, if you like, as you're the smallest."

Darbishire was no equestrian. "He won't bolt, will he?" he inquired uncertainly.

Mrs Hockin roared with laughter. "Good heavens, no! Considering he's spent the whole of his working life giving rides to children on the sands at Margate, he's not likely to behave like a bucking broncho now he's retired."

28

A leg-up from Jennings helped Darbishire to clamber on to his bare-backed mount where he sat, proud and triumphant, doing his best to look like a competitor at a gymkhana. Temple jerked on the rope and the party moved off, following Mrs Hockin down the path through the wood.

Jennings was curious to know more about their destination. This woman didn't fit in with his idea of what a seaside donkey proprietor should look like. "Is it a farm we're going to?" he asked her.

"Nothing like that, I'm afraid – nothing so grand," she replied as he fell into step beside her. "It's just a sort of geriatric ward for elderly animals." She noted his puzzled look and forestalled his question by going on, "Homeless cats, ownerless dogs, worn-out donkeys. You name it – we give it house-room." She laughed and shook her head. "It certainly isn't a farm. Any farmer who put up with my sort of livestock would be out of business in six weeks."

They were there in a matter of minutes. A home-made signboard nailed to a broken gate proclaimed *The Retreat*, and once past the barrier the boys found themselves in a paddock of long grass with a row of stables and outbuildings at the far end.

Close by the stables rose the chimneys of a house, and beyond that was a small, but thickly-wooded copse surrounded by more rough grazing land dotted with clumps of briar, gorse and brambles. The ground was untended and everywhere the grass was long and shrubs and bushes grew wild.

"It's all rather higgledy-piggledy, I'm afraid," Mrs

29

Hockin was saying as Darbishire slithered off the donkey, which wandered away to join three more of its kind browsing round a clump of thistles. "I do what I can, of course, but I've been on my own since my husband died and I sometimes feel I'm fighting a losing battle."

She was a talkative woman with a forthright manner, and by the time the party had crossed the paddock they had heard how she had converted a former smallholding into an animal sanctuary and now devoted her time and energy to the welfare of the inmates.

"Money's the big problem, of course," she went on as they drew near to the stables. "You'd never believe what some of these animals can put away at mealtimes. And apart from feeding, there's the question of making them keep to their own quarters. These fences are just a joke." She waved a hand at a frail erection of sagging chicken-wire which she laughingly described as the goat-pen. One of the goats had uprooted a length of netting and was cavorting around outside the enclosure trailing yards of chicken-wire from its horns.

"T't! Look at that!" Mrs Hockin tut-tutted in mild reproach. "My neighbour, Major Rudkin, explodes with rage whenever my goats get into his orchard. And the night the baby badgers wandered on to his croquet lawn – well, really!"

The stables and outhouses, built round a cobblestone square, were clearly in need of a builder's attention. Cracks in the brickwork, missing tiles and peeling paint underlined the fact that there was little money to spare for maintenance.

30

Not that the inhabitants of the sanctuary bothered about that! Sunning themselves on the cobblestones were seven dogs of different breeds and sizes who welcomed the visitors with a boisterous greeting that knocked Darbishire and Atkinson off their feet. Ensconced on roofs and window-ledges a dozen or more cats watched the proceedings with dignified calm.

There was plenty for the boys to see wherever they looked. Two monkeys were enjoying the run of a derelict stable next door to an old white horse fast asleep on its feet. Rabbit hutches, dovecotes and a duck pond were either in use or showing signs of recent occupation.

The boys spent the next half hour exploring the sanctuary and making friends with the animals which Mrs Hockin had taken into her care. All the cats were strays and the dogs had either been found wandering or had been brought to her by owners who could not cope with their pets. The donkeys and the aged horse she had bought from her slender resources to save them from work for which they were no longer suited. Despite their widely differing backgrounds, all the animals had one thing in common: they had come to live with Mrs Hockin because nobody else wanted them any more.

Jennings wandered off into the paddock where Venables, clutching a bunch of stale cabbages, was getting to know a goat.

"Hey, Jennings! Come over here," he called. "This old goat's actually eating out of my hand."

"That's more than I should want to do," said Jennings. "Still, goats aren't fussy, are they?"

He ducked as Venables threw a cabbage stalk at him, and then stayed to watch until shouts from the stable yard announced that the party was preparing to move on.

As the two boys rejoined the group, Mrs Hockin was directing Mr Carter back to the camp by a circular route.

"It'll mean your crossing Major Rudkin's land, of course, but there's a right of way, so don't be put off by his stupid notices about trespassers," she told him. "The major and I don't get on very well, I'm afraid. He regards most forms of wildlife as something to shoot at. Too trigger-happy by half, I call him. The wretched man can't even see a bullfinch without reaching for his gun."

Their way led them back across the paddock, over Mrs Hockin's rickety fences to a wood where the path was so overgrown that they had to make their way along in single file. Soon the path gave out altogether and they struggled on through briars and brambles that tore at their anoraks and whipped back in their faces.

"I bet it was just like this when Dr Livingstone was exploring Darkest Africa," Darbishire said after a while. "Impenetrable jungle where the foot of white man has never trod." He picked up a dead branch and held it like a rifle at the ready. In imagination he was an explorer in the tropics; lean, bronzed and fearless, facing the dangers of the unknown. He slipped back the safety-catch of his makeshift rifle. "Be prepared! Could be cannibal country," he threw out over his shoulder, speaking in the cool, laconic tones that seemed to go with the lean, bronzed features.

Jennings, walking just behind him, recognised the character and played up. "Keep your eyes skinned and be ready to stand your ground. If the natives are hostile, leave the talking to me. I speak their lingo."

"You do!" The lean explorer was impressed. "Swahili, I suppose, or would it be Zulu?"

"No – English!" Jennings pointed to a notice-board nailed to a tree: it said TRESPASSERS WILL BE PROSECUTED. A short distance away another board read PRIVATE, KEEP OUT. "Maybe they're not actually cannibals in these parts, but they don't sound very friendly."

The warning notices punctured Darbishire's fantasy like an arrow from the undergrowth. The lean, bronzed explorer faded and in his place was a fair-haired, bespectacled eleven-year-old looking slightly apprehensive. "Oh fish-hooks, I didn't know we were trespassing," he said, dropping his makeshift gun. "I hope we don't meet anybody."

His hopes were disappointed. Fifty yards further on the bushes thinned out and they came into a small clearing where a stocky, red-faced man in tweeds and a deer-stalker hat was waiting with a shotgun under his arm.

He stood scowling in silence as the party emerged from the undergrowth and then strode up to Mr Carter who was bringing up the rear. "Are you aware that this is private property?" he demanded.

33

Mr Carter, breathless from his struggles through the undergrowth, nodded briefly.

"Then what d'you think you're doing – trespassing on my land like a bunch of gypsies! Get back where you came from before I call the police." His tone was threatening, his manner hostile.

"Do you mind lowering that gun while we're talking?" Mr Carter said politely. "I take it that you're the landowner – Major Rudkin, I believe?"

The major acknowledged his identity with a grunt. "It's no business of yours whether I'm the landowner or not. This is private property and you've no right to be on it."

Mr Carter declined to be ruffled. "I'm not disputing the fact that this is your property. I would merely remind you that there's a public footpath across it from your neighbour's paddock to the main road."

"Public footpath!" The major snorted in derision and waved an arm at the almost impenetrable jungle surrounding them. "I see no footpath!"

"Nobody can *see* the footpath for the very good reason that it's been allowed to become overgrown," Mr Carter pointed out. "All the same, a right of way does exist and we're entitled to use it."

"You're entitled to do nothing of the sort. There's no right of way across my land."

By way of reply, Mr Carter produced an Ordnance Survey map of the district from his anorak pocket and pointed out the dotted line upholding the right of law-abiding pedestrians to walk across the property.

Major Rudkin waved the evidence aside. "That map's out of date," he objected.

"It's the latest edition. I bought it in the village yesterday," Mr Carter informed him. "I wouldn't have brought the boys this way without first making sure of my facts."

By this time the boys were standing together in a tight knot, following every word of the argument and feeling slightly embarrassed at the spectacle of Mr Carter's authority being called into question by this aggressive man with a gun.

As for the major, he was perfectly well aware that the right of way existed, and had always done his best to discourage people from using it. By obliterating the path, erecting barbed wire barriers and putting up notices he was able to intimidate most of the people who came that way and stop them enjoying their lawful rights.

He was, therefore, particularly annoyed with Mr Carter for proving him in the wrong. It was one thing to browbeat innocent wayfarers, and quite another to argue with the latest edition of the Ordnance Survey map. Even so, he made one more attempt to frustrate their journey. He said, "That map's no use if the path isn't there any more. You'll have to go back the way you've come." He jerked his thumb in the direction of *The Retreat*. "If that Hockin woman is fool enough to let people go trampling over her land, that's her business: but you're not going any further over *mine*."

Mr Carter ignored him and turned to the boys. "We're going on till we reach the road. We shall follow the route marked on the map," he announced. "I'll lead the way and you boys will follow in single file."

In silence the boys lined up behind their leader and followed him across the clearing.

The major said nothing. But, as they went, the boys were conscious of his furious glare following them until they were out of sight. When they were safely out of earshot, the boys' tongues were loosened.

"Coo, rotten old Major Trigger-Happy or whatever his name is! Still, he didn't get the better of us, did he, sir?" Venables observed.

"He would have done if we'd been by ourselves," Atkinson pointed out. "We wouldn't have had a hope without Sir to speak up for us."

Jennings looked at Darbishire and grinned. "I told you the natives were hostile. If it had *really* been cannibals he'd have had you in the pot ready for supper by now."

Darbishire smiled wanly. The encounter with the trigger-happy landowner had been acutely embarrassing to one of his peaceful temperament: he felt he'd explored enough jungles for one day.

A hundred yards further on they came to what had once been a stile leading to the road. It was typical of the major's methods that the stile had been barricaded with barbed wire and decorated with KEEP OUT notices to deter the public from entering his domain. The boys scrambled through, over and under the wire with slight damage to their jeans and then set off along the road leading back to the camp.

They had to wait at the flashing red lights of a level

crossing adjoining Southcombe Station for a train to go by. Shortly afterwards they left the road as it entered the village and climbed up the hill to the camp, where preparations for the midday meal were running behind schedule.

Bromwich was wedging a stone under one foot of the wobbling cooking-stove in the hope of improving its stability. Near at hand, Mr Wilkins, hot and flustered, was sprinkling tomato ketchup over the dried-up remains of some tinned casserole steak which had been charred to cinders in the frying-pan.

"Afraid we're running a bit late. We had an accident," Rumbelow greeted the hungry home-comers. "Bromwich left a soapy pot-scourer in the saucepan after the washing-up, and we didn't find out till we'd put the Brussels sprouts in for dinner."

The culprit looked up from his flint-wedging and added, "You should have seen the water! It came boiling up over the top, all pink and frothy. We had to throw the whole lot away: we thought you might notice the taste." He turned to Jennings. "How did you lot get on?"

"We had a fantastic time. We met an old lady with lots of animals called Mrs – er – Something-or-other and a ghastly old man with a gun called – er—" Jennings flipped his fingers to stir his memory, but it was no use. "T't! I can't remember their names now."

"Never mind anyway," said Bromwich, losing interest. "It doesn't really matter what their names were. I don't suppose you'll ever see them again."

"No, I don't suppose I shall," Jennings replied . . .
But as it happened he was wrong!

Chapter 4

Scene Change

Towards the end of the week Jennings wrote to his aunt.

"Dear Aunt Angela . . . We are having a lot of fun in camp and doing a lot of famous exploits. Mr Wilkins showed us how to build a bridge over a river, but there isn't a river here which is just as well as it collapsed when he tried it out. Also, Mr Wilkins' cooking was getting better, but not very much so now Mr Carter does it instead. We shall de-camp on Tuesday after breakfast, so please don't be late coming to fetch me or everybody else will have gone. I am looking forward to staying with you till Mum and Dad get back from Norway . . . Love, John."

Angela Birkinshaw, Jennings' favourite aunt, was a social worker who lived in a tall block of flats in south London. Though her duties left her with little spare time, she normally managed to visit her nephew once or twice each term and occasionally he would stay at her flat for a day or so during the holidays.

This time she had arranged for him to be her guest for longer than usual for his parents were not due back in England for another week. Mr Jennings, an engineer, had been sent abroad by his firm, taking his wife with him in the expectation of being home again by the start of the school holidays. But the work had taken longer than anyone had foreseen and they found themselves obliged to remain in Scandinavia until the job was finished. Thus, they were more than willing to accept Angela's offer to look after their son until they returned.

Miss Birkinshaw made a note in her diary to arrive in good time on the following Tuesday. She was glad to hear that the holiday under canvas was proving such a success.

It was, by any standards, a very successful camp – all the boys were agreed on that. In a week of varied activities they explored the Surrey countryside on foot and in the van. They enjoyed riotous sing-songs round the camp fire and – thanks to their camp duties – learned a great deal about coping with life in the open air.

The only near-disaster occurred one blowy afternoon when Darbishire lost control of Atkinson's kite which sailed away over the field and became entangled with the telephone wires on the road at the bottom of the hill. Apart from the loss of the kite there was some doubt as to whether the accident had severed telephonic communication between Southcombe and the rest of the world; and telephone engineers had to be summoned to free the wires and make sure that all was well.

Aunt Angela arrived at ten o'clock on Tuesday morning just as the big tent was being folded and stowed on the roof-rack of the mini-bus. Her arrival coincided with that of several parents who had arranged to collect their boys at the site, and the next quarter of an hour was taken up by last-minute packing and lively farewells.

"Goodbye, sir. Thanks ever so much for everything," Jennings said on taking leave of Mr Wilkins. "Hope you have a great holiday. See you next term, sir."

The master sighed in mock resignation as he shook hands. "I'm hoping to have a very quiet and restful holiday from now on," he said. "No noisy third-formers and definitely no cooking."

"Don't worry, sir. The cooking wasn't as bad as all that – well, only sometimes."

Mr Wilkins ignored the compliment. "And as for your saying, 'See you next term' in that bright-eyed and bushy-tailed tone of voice, allow me to point out, Jennings, that there's no need to make it sound as though it's something to look forward to!"

Gaitskell Court in south-east London, was a tall block of flats on a housing estate comprising four similar blocks built round a central courtyard. Aunt Angela lived at Flat 64 on the eighth level, less than half way up the building but high enough to command a panoramic view stretching from the hills in the southern

41

suburbs to the office blocks of central London beyond
the Thames. The housing estate was a modern development in a densely-populated district and Angela found
Gaitskell Court a convenient place to live as it was
central for her work.

The journey from Southcombe was uneventful, and
shortly after midday Miss Birkinshaw's car was crawling along the High Street in the heavy London traffic.
It was raining and the outlook through the windscreen
was depressing and unchanging. The multiple shops
and supermarkets were replicas of those they had been
passing for the last five miles and the view down almost
every side street was of filling-stations offering car tyres
at staggering discounts.

"I hope you'll find enough to do while you're at the
flat, John," Aunt Angela said doubtfully. "There's not
an awful lot going on in these parts to interest someone
your age."

"Don't worry; I'll find plenty to keep me busy,"
Jennings assured her. "I'm never bored. I've never
been bored in my life."

The car turned in through the entrance to the estate
and drove across to the parking area. A grey-haired
man in a boiler-suit was emptying litter bins.

"That's Mr Fagg," Aunt Angela said, waving to him
through the car window. "He's new here since your
last visit."

The caretaker acknowledged the wave and walked
over to the car as it came to a stop. He stooped to
speak through the car window.

"You'll have to watch your step, Miss Birkinshaw,"

he said solemnly. "Those two old girls on Level Five are out for your blood."

Angela looked puzzled. "What have I done now?"

"Ah, it's not what you've done – it's what you *haven't* done," Mr Fagg went on. His voice was a rich gravelly cockney, his expression gloomy and his whole bearing that of a man prepared for the worst – and never surprised when the worst happened. "It's that petition they got up about the kids making a row in the court-yard. You never signed it, did you!"

"Of course I didn't! The children have got to play somewhere, and where else if not out here?" Aunt Angela's gaze swept the tarmac where a group of youngsters were playing football at the far end. "I admit some of them get a bit noisy at times, but I'm sure it doesn't disturb Mrs Pratt and Mrs Plumrose. They're too high up to hear much on the fourth floor."

Mr Fagg nodded. "Thought as I'd tip you the wink. As like as not they'll be up to see you about it. They've been on at me all the week, as though I'd got nothing better to do. T't! We get all sorts here, don't we!" Though his face remained gloomy there was the hint of a twinkle in his eye which showed on which side his sympathies lay.

As they went up in the lift, Jennings said, "What are you going to do if these people come and ask you to sign their petition?"

Aunt Angela considered, "I shall be tactful. I shall offer them a cup of tea and try to talk them out of it."

"You don't have to sign if you don't want to. Couldn't you just say 'no'?"

"That *wouldn't* be very tactful. They're my neighbours, you see; and when you live in a small community like a block of flats, everybody's got to consider the needs of other people."

Number 64 Gaitskell Court was identical in design to all the other flats in the block: the living-room and the kitchen overlooking the courtyard were separated from two bedrooms and a bathroom by a hall which ran the length of the apartment.

They had lunch in the kitchen. When the meal was over, Angela said, "Any plans for this afternoon?"

Jennings knew what he wanted to do. "First of all, Auntie, if you'll lend me your binoculars, I want to go up to the top of the block and get my bearings."

This was always the first thing he did whenever he visited the flat. The view from the roof fascinated him: the teeming streets and crawling traffic so far below; raise the sights a little and there was the television mast at Crystal Palace, football grounds, church spires, distant trains and mile after mile of grey slate roofs stretching as far as the skyline. With all this below him he could pretend he was a pilot bringing his aircraft into Heathrow airport.

Aunt Angela produced the binoculars. "Don't play about with the lift buttons on the way up," she said. "People have got stuck between floors doing that."

Jennings assured her he wouldn't. "Anyway, I'm not going up in the lift. I'm going down to street level first."

"Funny place to admire the view from the roof!"

"Ah, but I want to walk all the way up this time. I'm going to count how many stairs there are altogether."

Angela laughed. "That'll keep you out of mischief for an hour or two."

Counting the number of stairs in a tower block of flats is a pastime that soon loses its appeal. However, Jennings persisted, taking little rests at each landing to inspect the view through the binoculars. When he was four flights up it occurred to him that, as there was the same number of stairs to each flight, the obvious way to find the total was to multiply this figure by the number of storeys in the building.

But this would have been too easy! Climbing the staircase was an achievement: he must not shrink from conquering the concrete mountain step by step. Up he went . . . Ninety-six, ninety-seven, ninety-eight . . .

Jennings was peering out from the eighth level window when the sound of ascending footsteps was wafted up from below. He was surprised. Why should anyone apart from himself (and *he* was doing it for a challenge) want to tire themselves out on the stairs when the lift was in working order?

He looked over the banister rail down the well of the staircase. Two floors below he could see the slim figure of a girl in a navy-blue school raincoat. There was something stealthy in her movements as she mounted the stairs. Twice she looked back as though making sure that she was not being followed: and when her arrival at the next landing coincided with the stopping of the lift, she darted back to the bend in the stairs to avoid being seen when the lift door slid open.

45

Jennings was puzzled, and stood watching her stealthy ascent after the lift had gone. Clearly, she was unaware that she was being observed from above. He'd better reveal his presence, he thought, if only to warn her that she was not alone. So, as she came up to the next half landing, he leaned over the banisters and said, "Hullo!"

The effect was dramatic. The girl gave a squeak of fright and leapt like a startled rabbit. Then she looked up and saw that the speaker belonged to her own age-group. She relaxed a little and said, "Whew! You didn't half put the wind up me. I thought you were a grown-up – Mrs Pratt or somebody."

He thought of saying, "Why, do I look like Mrs Pratt or somebody?" but the strained look on her face warned him that she wasn't in the mood for jocular remarks. So he just said, "Sorry, I didn't mean to scare you. I just wondered what was going on."

He judged the girl to be about his own age, though she was not as tall. She was thin and wiry with dark hair, large brown eyes and a wide mouth. She came up and joined him on the landing.

"Had to get home without being spotted." The girl unbuttoned her raincoat at the top, revealing a small mongrel puppy hidden beneath. "It's him. If they find out I've got him, he'll be out on his ear. Me, too, I shouldn't wonder. Both out on our ears."

Jennings was puzzled. "Why?"

"It's the rule, isn't it! No pets. Not allowed animals in the flats. Didn't you know?"

"No, I didn't. I'm only staying here." He glanced

The girl unbuttoned her raincoat at the top, revealing a small mongrel puppy hidden beneath

with interest at the small black snout sniffing at a rain-coat button. "He's only a small pet, though. Not like an Irish wolfhound or something."

She laughed. "If the housing department says 'no pets', it doesn't matter whether they're goldfish or gorillas. It's 'no pets', full stop."

The sound of voices floated up the well of the stair-case and she quickly tucked the puppy back under her raincoat and started off again, up the stairs. "I can't hang about talking, or I'll be in trouble."

"Anything I can do to help?" Jennings called after her.

"I don't know. There might be. Come into my place if you like and we'll talk about it."

Jennings needed no urging. He caught her up before she reached the next landing where she stopped at a flat opposite the lift. A name-plate on the door read *No. 72 G. J. Sparrow.*

The girl led the way along the hall and into the kitchen, where she put the puppy down in a cardboard carton. Then she said, "First of all, whose side are you on?"

Jennings looked blank. "I'm not on anybody's side that I know of. I told you I don't live here. I'm just staying with my aunt in Number 64 – the flat below this one."

"Miss Birkinshaw's, isn't it?" She seemed satisfied. "*She's* all right. Not like Mrs Plumrose and all that lot. What's your name, then?"

"Jennings."

"I can't call you that. Haven't you got a first name?"

Jennings nodded. "John. I'm only Jennings at school."

"School doesn't count. It's the holidays now." She took off her raincoat and dropped it on a chair. "My name's Emma."

"Emma Sparrow," Jennings corrected. "I saw it on the front door." He knelt down and stroked the puppy which was trying to scramble out of its makeshift bed. "And if you're not allowed to have pets, how did you get him past the caretaker?"

"I smuggled him. That's why I always use the stairs. I daren't take him in the lift."

Jennings was staggered at the physical effort involved. "But you can't carry him up and down a hundred and thirty-five stairs every time he wants to go out. He'll be too big soon, anyway, and then what?"

Emma sighed and hunched her thin shoulders. "That's the problem. I'm pretty sure Mrs Pratt's got her suspicions already because she saw me walking him out in the street. And if she reports it, old Fagg will be up here to search the flat and he'll find all the other animals, as well."

"All the other . . . !" Jennings gaped at her. Was this undersized waif of a girl running a secret wildlife reserve on the ninth level of a municipal block of flats!

Emma led the way into a bedroom across the hall. A kitten was washing itself on the rug and taking no notice of two lively gerbils scampering in a cage on the bedside chair. In a box on the chest of drawers a hedgehog was fast asleep; a tortoise was motionless on the hearth rug; goldfish swam in a tank on the window-sill.

Jennings whistled in surprise. Emma had certainly got problems if she was hoping to conceal this illegal collection of dumb friends from the watchful eye of the borough housing department. "Where did you get them from?" he asked.

"I didn't get them – or rather I didn't *mean* to. They got me, if you see what I mean. You see what happened was—"

As the tale was unfolded it became clear that Emma's troubles stemmed from her devotion to animals and her readiness to shelter them in distress. The kitten and the puppy were strays which she had found in the street. The gerbils had belonged to a school friend who was unable to give them proper protection from the family cat. The goldfish had been a prize at a fairground shooting range, won by a youth who didn't want them and was about to tip them down a drain when Emma intervened. As she sat perched on the edge of the bed telling him all about it, Jennings couldn't help thinking that Emma Sparrow in her rôle of self-appointed animal welfare officer had a great deal in common with Mrs Hockin in Southcombe.

"But what about the hedgehog?" he queried. "You didn't find *him* mooching up and down the High Street looking for lodgings!"

The hedgehog was an exception, Emma explained. It appeared that a girl from a neighbouring housing block had found it lying injured by the roadside in a Surrey lane; but having brought it all the way home in the boot of the family car, her pleas for its survival had been frustrated by the housing department's anti-livestock rule. Emma, acting on impulse and with little thought for the consequences, had offered to nurse it back to health.

And Emma's parents? Jennings persisted. What did they think of this unlawful menagerie in the bedroom?

Emma pulled a face and rolled her large brown eyes. "Well, they're on my side, really, but they've said it's got to stop," she admitted. "I've promised to find homes for them all, but it's not going to be easy. Nobody in the flats can take them because of the rule, and if Mr Fagg finds out and reports it to the housing department—"

She broke off as the front door bell rang, loud and shrill. "Help, this could be him now," she exclaimed, all her agitation flooding back at the horrifying prospect. "I bet that Pratt woman's put him on my track. What am I going to do if he wants to come in and search the place!"

"Don't answer the door," Jennings suggested.

"But he knows I'm in. He saw me in the courtyard just now. He might even have spotted I'd got the puppy under my coat."

This was no time to discuss what the caretaker might – or might not – have seen. "Better see who it is," Jennings advised. "You don't have to let him in if your mother and father are out. And don't panic," he went on as the door bell rang again. "It probably isn't the caretaker, anyway!"

But it was!

Leaving Jennings on guard in the bedroom, Emma hurried into the hall and opened the front door a few cautious inches.

" 'Afternoon," said Mr Fagg in his deep, gravelly voice, "I'd like a word with your parents, if I may."

"They're not in," Emma told him, doing her best to sound unconcerned. "Mum's still on duty at the hospital and Dad – er – well I'm not expecting him back from the fire station, just yet."

"H'm! Perhaps I could come in and wait, then."

Emma gulped slightly and took a grip on herself. "I don't usually let people in without my parents knowing."

Mr Fagg nodded in approval. "Of course not! Too many strangers hanging round the flats as it is. But it's a bit different in my case, isn't it? Seeing as I'm in charge of the block, as you might say, you can hardly call me a stranger."

Emma was speechless with indecision. She couldn't let him in, but to persist with her objections might increase his suspicions still further.

He noticed her embarrassment and said, "Fair enough! I've got a few jobs to get on with, up here. I daresay your mother will be back by the time I'm through."

He was carrying a carpenter's bag and some panes of glass, and as Emma shut the door she saw him preparing to start work on re-glazing a broken window overlooking the adjacent block.

Jennings poked his head out of the small bedroom. "Has he gone?"

"Yes, but he's still on the landing. He's waiting for my mum to come home. Then he'll be in to search the flat." Her lip trembled; she was on the point of tears. "They'll take them all away and have them destroyed. Either that or turn them loose, so they'll get killed whatever happens."

It was not often in the course of his eleven years that John Christopher Timothy Jennings had been called upon to come to the aid of damsels in distress. Now, however, there was no mistaking the summons. He must *do* something!

For some moments he frowned in thought. Then he said, "There's only one way out. We'll have to smuggle them all out of your flat until Mr Fagg's finished searching."

Emma stared at him blankly. "That's not possible. Where could we put them?"

"In my Aunt Angela's flat, of course. *She's* not being searched. Mind you, they'll have to come back again when he's gone, but at least it'll give you a breathing space."

The blank look faded and Emma's eyes sparkled with hope. "D'you think we really could! It'd only be for a little while and I'll find proper homes for them tomorrow, I promise I will."

With Miss Birkinshaw's co-operation taken for granted, the plan sounded feasible. It was only when they came to discuss ways and means that they realised what snags lay ahead.

The caretaker's presence on the landing meant that staircase and lift were barred to them as an escape route. It would be useless waiting for him to finish his work and go downstairs, for the broken window might well be an excuse for him to keep the entrance of Flat 72 under observation.

Just to make sure, Jennings made a cautious survey through the letter-box. As expected, the situation was grave.

"He's got everything all spread out – glass, putty, paint, tools. He's perishing well going to stay on guard till your mum gets back. Just shows how suspicious he is."

Emma flipped her fingers in despair. "It's hopeless. We'll have to call it off. There's just no way of getting them past him. And even if we—"

She stopped and stared at Jennings in puzzled wonder. He was dancing a little jig of inspiration on the rug – to the alarm of the tortoise who hurriedly retired under the bed.

"I've got it!" he cried excitedly. "It came to me in a flash. We'll let them down out of the window."

"Eh!"

"Or rather, *you'll* let them down, and I'll be down at Aunt Angela's kitchen window to take them in."

Emma was stunned with the boldness of the plan. "Yes, but what if—"

"Don't argue," said Jennings, firmly taking command. "If you want to save the pets you haven't got any choice. Just do as I say."

Emma glanced at him uncertainly. She wasn't used to taking orders from strange boys no older than herself. She thought his scheme was crazy, impractical – frightening, even. But what else could they do!

Finally she said, "OK, then. Only I don't like it. I hope to goodness you know what you're doing."

Together they moved the livestock from Emma's bedroom across the hall to the kitchen. Jennings opened the window and looked out. Aunt Angela's kitchen window was immediately beneath him, only a few feet below. Lowering the animals to safety should present no problem, provided they could find suitable containers.

Emma produced a length of clothes line and her father's fishing basket. "We can strap the lid down: they can't possibly fall out," she said as she assembled the equipment on the kitchen table. "The gerbils will be all right in their cage – we can tie the line through the wires. And the goldfish—" She wrinkled her nose in doubt. "We can't let the fish tank down on a clothes line. There's nothing to tie it to."

Jennings considered the point. "You'll have to decant them into a milk jug or something with a handle. They'll be all right: it's only down to the next floor."

They spent a few minutes discussing details. Then Jennings said, "Right! Stand by for orders to lower away. I'm going down to take charge at the reception base. And don't worry," he called back as he hurried out into the hall. "This is one of my guaranteed fool-proof plans. It can't possibly go wrong!"

Chapter 5

The Best Laid Plans

Despite his reassuring words to Emma, Jennings felt a twinge of anxiety as he went down the stairs to Aunt Angela's flat. It was all very well devising ingenious plans *at school*: there, at least, he knew what hazards he was likely to meet. But here in Gaitskell Court he was in unknown territory, liable to face dangers that he couldn't assess.

Mr Fagg hadn't even glanced up from his work when he had passed him on the landing. But that was natural enough. Whatever suspicions the caretaker may have had about Emma, he couldn't know that a secret ally had now come to her aid.

Having no latchkey, Jennings rang the bell at Flat No. 64 and Aunt Angela let him in.

"Well, did you find out how many stairs there were?" she asked as he put the binoculars down on the hall table.

He'd forgotten about counting the stairs. "Actually, I didn't get right up to the top," he said. "You see, I met a girl called Emma Sparrow from Flat 72 and—" He paused, thinking hard. It had only just occurred to

him that he had made his plans for the evacuation of
the animals without consulting Aunt Angela. Supposing she raised objections! She was entitled to. After
all, it was *her* flat!

"You see, Emma's in a spot of trouble and I said I'd
help her," Jennings went on. "There's isn't much time,
but I ought to tell you about it first, because—"

"D'you mind telling me later," Aunt Angela broke
in, and it was obvious that her mind was on other
matters. "I've got my hands full of Mrs Plumrose and
Mrs Pratt at the moment. They've come to see me
about that petition."

Jennings was horrified. Inquisitive neighbours presented a complication that he had not foreseen. But it
was too late, now, to alter his plans.

"Where are they now?" he asked.

"In the living-room, of course. Where else! I shan't
sign their petition, though. I'll try to talk them out of
it over a neighbourly cup of tea." So saying, Angela
went back to cope with her unwelcome guests while
Jennings hurried into the kitchen to put the animal
rescue project into action.

Emma was ready and waiting at her post when he
poked his head out of the kitchen window. "Stand by
to take in refugees! Goldfish coming down first," she
called out.

Jennings signalled for silence with a finger to his lips.
Raised voices were bound to attract the attention of
the visitors in the adjoining room.

First over the sill came a pint-sized milk jug swinging
like a pendulum as it was lowered into space on the

end of the clothes line. When it was nearly within his reach it bumped against the brickwork just above his head; but a moment later he was able to reach out and pull the line into the safety of the kitchen.

To his dismay Jennings found that the impact had cracked the jug which was leaking water all over the floor and would soon be empty. Quickly, he untied the line and took the jug over to the sink where he gently deposited the goldfish in the washing-up bowl. By the time he had topped up the water level, the fishing basket was dangling on the clothes line outside the window.

The new arrival was the tortoise. Where could he put it? Not on the floor in case it wandered. He'd find suitable containers for them all later on, he decided, but for the time being the tortoise would have to be content with stretching its neck on the lid of the washing machine.

Jennings went back to the window and waited for the next occupant of the basket to start its descent. Emma seemed to be taking a long time buckling the strap.

"Quick as you can!" Jennings urged in a whisper as loud as he dared. "We can't take all day over this!"

She grinned down at him from her window. "OK! Hedgehog taking off next. Mind how you handle him."

"I shan't prick my fingers. I'll get something to wrap round him."

"It's not your fingers I'm worried about – it's my hedgehog: he's not better yet from his road accident. You've got to treat him like an invalid."

The invalid appeared quite comfortable after its journey through space. With a tea-towel to protect his hands, Jennings lifted the prickly creature out of the basket and set it down on the kitchen table.

Once more the basket was hauled aloft. It had just disappeared from view when the door opened and Aunt Angela came into the kitchen.

"I'm just going to put the kettle on," she began. "The good ladies are a *leetle* bit upset because I won't sign their petition, so I thought a cup of tea would—" The words tailed away as her eye lighted upon the hedgehog asleep on the table. "Goodness, what on earth's going on here?"

Her nephew gave her an apologetic smile. "I tried to tell you about it when I came in, only you were too busy," he explained. "I promised Emma Sparrow I'd keep them out of the way while they're searching her flat."

"Searching her flat! Who – the police?"

"No – the caretaker. It's this rule about not keeping animals. She's – sort of – accidentally got a few pets – quite by chance, of course. She's going to find homes for them as soon as she can – honestly."

Angela's gaze strayed away from the hedgehog and came to rest upon the tortoise doing its neck-stretching exercises on the washing machine.

"I'm sorry, John, but this is asking for trouble," she said. "We mustn't encourage Emma to break the rules like this. There's a clause in the tenancy agreement that says—"

"It's only for now, Auntie. She's going to take them back again, later. They'll all be gone by tonight."

"Tonight, yes! But what about now! I've got Mrs Plumrose and Mrs Pratt in the next room, don't forget."

"It'll be all right if they stay there," Jennings assured her. But even as he spoke, he realised that the worst was about to happen.

Shrill feminine voices sounded beyond the door and the next moment the ladies in question marched into the room, anxious to seize any excuse for snooping round their neighbour's kitchen. As they crossed the threshold, Jennings covered the hedgehog with the tea-towel and put a plastic vegetable colander over the tortoise.

"We thought as we'd come along and help," announced Mrs Plumrose. "Didn't think it right, leaving you to make the tea all by yourself."

She was a stout woman, well past middle age with dewlaps merging into a double chin that gave her the appearance of an elderly Bassett hound.

In contrast, Mrs Pratt was tall and skinny with a long, narrow-shaped head that put Jennings in mind of a costermonger's pony. Her voice retained a peevish note even when she was doing her best to sound agreeable. She glanced round the kitchen hoping to spot something to grumble about to Mrs Plumrose later on; but thanks to Jennings' presence of mind with tea-towel and colander she could find nothing amiss.

"I must say I always enjoy my cup of tea, afternoons," she began chattily. "And a nice cup, mornings, too, of course. So as soon as you went to put the kettle on, I thought to myself, I thought—"

"It's very kind of you both, but I don't need any help, really." Aunt Angela was tense with apprehension. She was annoyed with her nephew for involving her in what could well be an embarrassing situation. Mrs Pratt and Mrs Plumrose, busybodies both, were always quick to spread gossip and stir up trouble. And here was her nephew giving them a topic of conversation that would keep their tongues wagging for weeks. She *must* get rid of them before they found out what was going on!

"I'd much rather you went back to the living-room," she urged. "My nephew and I will make the tea, won't we John!"

The visitors noticed Jennings for the first time, but obviously didn't think much of him as a potential tea-maker.

"Wouldn't dream of letting you do all the work, Miss Birkinshaw," said Mrs Pratt. "Lend a helping hand, that's what I always say."

The helping hand picked up the kettle from the stove and carried it to the sink. But it never got as far as turning on the tap, for at that moment a blood-curdling scream rang out and Mrs Pratt staggered back from the sink with horror in her eyes.

"Aaagh!" she cried. "The washing-up bowl! It's full of fish!"

Mrs Plumrose on the far side of the room was slow to understand what the fuss was about. "Nothing wrong with a nice bit of fish," she observed. "We're having fish for supper, tonight, too. I got a nice bit of halibut at the supermarket this morning and I thought I'd shallow-fry it with a drop of—"

"No – not halibut! Goldfish!" squawked Mrs Pratt.

Mrs Plumrose shook her head. "You can't shallow-fry goldfish," she said. "Shrimps perhaps or even—"

"I'm not talking about *dead* fish. This lot's alive. Swimming about all over the bowl." Mrs Pratt nerved herself to take another look. "Ugh! Yeuch! It's proper put me off filling the kettle. I couldn't go near that sink again. Not with all those fish."

Angela did her best to cool the situation. "It's all right, Mrs Pratt – nothing to worry about," she said reassuringly. "Just a few pet goldfish. They belong to one of the children."

"*Pet* goldfish!" Mrs Pratt bridled with righteous concern. "No right to be here, they haven't. You know the tenancy agreement, Miss Birkinshaw. No pets allowed."

This was ridiculous, Jennings thought! "Oh, but you can't call goldfish pets," he protested. "Not like – er—" He was about to say cats or dogs until he remembered that the kitten and the puppy in the flat above might be arriving at any moment. "Well, I mean, you can't teach them tricks or take them for a walk, can you!"

"That's as maybe," said Mrs Pratt with a sniff.

Mrs Plumrose was more interested in a cup of tea than in arguments about taking goldfish for walks. Hoping to speed up the proceedings she took the teapot down from the plate rack and put it on the table . . . In doing so, her hand brushed against the tea-towel.

"Aaagh!" Once more a hoarse cry rent the air, start-ling the other occupants of the room who were astounded that such an eerie sound could have forced its way through Mrs Plumrose's vocal chords.

"There's something under the tea-towel. Something alive. It moved. Ugh! Take it away!" she cried.

Again, Aunt Angela tried to pacify her guests. "Don't get upset, Mrs Plumrose," she said soothingly. "It won't hurt you. It's only a hedgehog."

As though to confirm this statement a small black snout and a spiny head poked out from beneath the tea-towel, sniffed the air and then withdrew. Gasping with horror and shock, Mrs Plumrose sank down on to a kitchen stool which creaked ominously under her weight. "It moved! It had spikes all over. I felt them," she said faintly.

Her protest was taken up by Mrs Pratt who clearly held Aunt Angela responsible for this sudden infes-tation of wildlife. "I'm surprised, Miss Birkinshaw, really I am," she said, sniffing with disapproval. "This has always been a respectable block of flats. No ani-mals, no noisy children, no—"

Her words were lost in another shriek from Mrs Plumrose who was pointing at the window with trem-bling fingers. "Look! look!" she cried. "There! Outside the window. Something frightful."

All heads turned to the window where a wire cage occupied by two lively gerbils was dangling in space on the end of a clothes line.

Jennings avoided Aunt Angela's eye. There was nothing *he* could do about it; and nobody could blame Emma who had no means of knowing what was happening in the flat below.

For some seconds the visitors were too paralysed with shock to do anything but point and gibber. Then Mrs Pratt found her voice.

"Look what's in the cage," she shrieked. "*Rats!*"

Her cry was echoed by Mrs Plumrose. "Rats! Rats at the window, trying to get in. Keep them off! Take them away! Quick."

"They're not rats – they're gerbils," Jennings pointed out.

"I don't care what they are – they're horrible; I can't stand any more of this." Mrs Pratt, feeling faint, leant against the washing machine for support. The next second she leapt back as though stung, for the plastic vegetable colander started to move across the top of the machine without any visible means of propulsion. It wouldn't have helped matters, Jennings decided, to explain that the tortoise was feeling restive.

Mrs Pratt was almost beside herself. "Fish in the wash-bowl! Hedgehogs in the tea-towels! Rats tapping at the window!" Her voice grew shrill with panic. "Come on, Mrs Plumrose, we're not stopping here. We'll go and report this at once!"

Jennings looked down at his feet as the front door slammed behind the retreating visitors.

"Sorry, Auntie," he said.

Mr Fagg had finished re-glazing the window and was

packing up his tools when a babble of protesting voices rang out on the landing below. He recognised the voices only too well, for scarcely a day passed without a complaint of some sort from Mrs Plumrose or Mrs Pratt.

This time, however, there was an urgency in their tones that prompted him to investigate, instead of running for cover as he usually did. So, leaning over the banisters he called, "What's the trouble, ladies? Building on fire, or something?"

They swung round and looked upwards at the sound of his voice.

"Quick! Come quick, it's urgent," cried Mrs Pratt, round-eyed with horror. "We've got rats in the flats, Mr Fagg! . . . Rats in the flats!"

They hurried up the stairs towards him, breathless with exertion and incoherent of speech.

"It was dreadful, horrible, frightful!" Mrs Pratt gasped as they met him on the bend of the stairs. "Miss Birkinshaw's kitchen! She's got wash in the fishing-up bowl. All alive and swimming about. I couldn't bring myself to go near it."

"Yes, and the tea-towel, too," wheezed Mrs Plumrose. "That great spiky creature with long spikes sticking out all over. It was alive; it looked at me! Ugh!"

Mr Fagg was out of his depth. He could guess what a fishing-up bowl was, but the spikes baffled him. "A porcupine, was it?" he hazarded.

"I don't know. It might have been," Mrs Plumrose said with a shudder. "They said something about hedgehogs, but you can't believe all you hear these days, can you?"

"And the rats, Mrs Plumrose," her neighbour urged. "Tell him about the rats."

"*You* tell him, Mrs Pratt. You saw them too."

"No, *you* tell him, Mrs Plumrose. You saw them first."

The caretaker was about to suggest tossing a coin to decide the matter when Mrs Plumrose graciously accepted the rôle of narrator. Now that the shock of discovering the creatures was beginning to wear off, she was revelling in the fact that she had a spine-chilling story to tell.

"Well, there they were, tapping at the window," she began in suitably outraged tones. "They were trying to get in, you see, snarling and gnashing their teeth. Great monstrous things! I screamed; I couldn't help it. I said—"

"Hey, hold on a minute," Mr Fagg interposed in disbelief. "You saw these rats *outside* the window?"

"That's right. Great monstrous—"

"It's eight levels up, you know!"

This was not the moment, Mrs Plumrose decided, for anyone to spoil a good story by querying the details. "That's where we saw them," she asserted. "Mrs Pratt will tell you the same. Outside the window, they were. Hovering! . . . Waiting their chance!"

Mr Fagg restrained himself from laughing out loud. Indeed, his expression grew more solemn as he goaded the narrator of this incredible story into even wilder flights of fancy.

"Marvellous, isn't it," he said in flat, deadpan tones. "The wonders of nature! Flying rats!"

"No. Not flying – dangling. Hanging in space."

"Flapping their wings at you, were they! T't-t't-t't!"

"They didn't have wings," Mrs Pratt said testily. "They were in a cage."

"I see. In a cage. Hovering in space a hundred feet up in the air!"

Mrs Pratt and Mrs Plumrose exchanged glances. It was beginning to dawn on them that the caretaker entertained doubts about the truth of their story. Mrs Pratt said, "That's what we saw, as true as I'm standing here."

"Yes, yes, of course," he assured her with mock gravity. "And what about the porcupine? Was he out there with them doing a parachute jump?"

This was too much for Mrs Pratt. Waving a skinny forefinger at the caretaker, she cried, "Don't you try to be funny with us, Mr Fagg. It's your duty to see the rules are kept in these flats. No pets – that's the rule! And here's Miss Birkinshaw keeping all those dreadful creatures in her kitchen. We might have been attacked. Lucky to get out of the place alive, we were."

Although he had no idea what the ladies were talking about, he would have to go and investigate, Mr Fagg decided. Indeed, as caretaker of the block he had no option but to deal with any complaint that was brought to his notice. But this one was so fantastic that it was beyond reason. The old girls must be clean round the Ponders End!

"Fair enough, then. I'll have a word with Miss

Birkinshaw," he agreed, making his way down the stairs: but when he reached Flat 64 the ladies were hard at his heels, anxious not to miss any sensational developments.

This was the last thing he wanted. "No need for you to come in, ladies. I'll handle this myself," he said firmly.

"Oh, but we want to know what's going on," Mrs Pratt protested. "It was us who reported it, don't forget."

Mr Fagg pursed his lips and frowned. "Ah, but what about the danger! Those creatures you were on about – vampire rats and man-eating porcupines, or whatever! Could be lethal."

The ladies' enthusiasm wilted. "Well, perhaps we'd better not then," Mrs Plumrose decided, and rang for the lift. "I dare say we shall hear all about it afterwards."

"I'm sure you will," the caretaker agreed. Turning away, he added under his breath, "There's not much that goes on in these flats that you two nosey-parkers *don't* get to hear about, I'd say!"

Chapter 6

Heated Argument

Emma almost wept with frustration when Jennings came up to her flat to report that the plan had misfired. She had guessed that something must be amiss when the gerbils' cage was left dangling for so long without attention, but she had no inkling of the cause of the delay.

"Everything was going all right until those two old women came barging into the kitchen," said Jennings, recounting the tale of woe. "Old Fagg would never have known about it otherwise."

Emma nodded miserably. "And where is he now?"

"Old Fagg? He's down in Aunt Angela's kitchen. He wants to see you, so I said I'd come up and tell you."

Tense with apprehension, they made their way down to the flat on the lower floor. Mr Fagg was drinking a cup of tea and watching the antics of the gerbils scampering round their cage.

Emma swallowed hard and said, "Good afternoon, Mr Fagg," in a voice that was barely audible.

"Good afternoon *again*, young Emma," he returned,

looking up from the gerbils. "It's less than an hour ago since we had a little chat on your doorstep. Remember?"

"Yes, I know. Sorry," she mumbled.

The caretaker shook his head in puzzled wonder. "What have you been up to, then? What's it all about?"

She told him about her menagerie of waifs and strays (including the puppy and the kitten still in the flat above). There was no need to explain the reasons for secrecy. Mr Fagg knew the housing department's regulations better than anyone else.

Jennings listened with a rising sense of guilt. If he hadn't proposed his ill-fated plan, Emma wouldn't be in her present predicament.

"Look, it's all my fault really," he broke in halfway through her confession. "I helped her to smuggle the animals out. We were going to hide them down here until you'd searched her flat."

The caretaker's eyebrows shot up in astonishment. "Searched her flat!" he echoed. "What made you think I was going to do anything of the sort?"

"Well, weren't you? You said you were just waiting for her parents to come home."

"That's right. I wanted a word with them about the next meeting of the tenant's association," Mr Fagg agreed. He permitted himself a wan smile. "I'd no cause to search the place, though, had I? I didn't know then what I know now."

So he *hadn't* known about the animals! Jennings could have kicked himself. All that planning! All that trouble for nothing! Of course, if it hadn't been for

Emma's guilty conscience leading her to think that the net was closing in when it wasn't – but there was nothing to be gained by thinking along those lines. The plan had misfired; the truth was out, and that was that!

Mr Fagg frowned and said, "So what have you got to say for yourselves?"

"I'm sorry about the rules, really I am, but what else could I do?" Emma defended herself. "You see, the dog followed me in from the street and wouldn't go away and—"

"You didn't happen to feed him, by any chance?" the caretaker inquired.

"Well, only a bit. I had to. He was hungry."

"M'yes! And the next day, I suppose, the hedgehog followed you home on a bicycle and sat up and begged for a biscuit!"

"No, not exactly. You see, a girl at school—"

"All right, all right. I don't want their life stories. However you came by them, they've all got to go – and quickly."

"Oh yes, of course," Emma agreed. "Just give me a couple of weeks and—"

"Couple of weeks!" Mr Fagg was scandalised. "Are you joking! They're going tonight!" Then he saw the troubled look in her large brown eyes – and relented. He'd no business to let his head be ruled by his heart, he told himself severely, but on the other hand how could the girl possibly find a home for the creatures without notice! "Well, tomorrow, then," he conceded.

"But that gives us no time at all," Jennings argued. "First of all we've got to—"

"All right then – Thursday."

"But—"

"Thursday," boomed Mr Fagg, hardening his heart in accordance with the housing department's regulations. "And don't try to come the old soft soap over me. T't! You kids will get me the sack."

He put his teacup down and rose to his feet. "Now listen! You've got forty-eight hours to get rid of the whole boiling menagerie. I don't want to be hard on you: I'm trying to be fair. But if I find so much as a whisker of an animal in or around Flat 72 on Thursday night, it'll mean a full report to the manager of the borough housing department. And you won't want that!"

He strode from the room; and a moment later they heard him talking to Aunt Angela in the hall. Then the front door slammed behind him.

Emma stood staring into space, twisting her fingers and biting her lower lip. She said, "They can turn you out of the flats for breaking the rules, you know; and what's my mum and dad going to say when they get back and—"

"Don't worry, Emma," Jennings consoled her. "I expect everything will be all right."

It wasn't a helpful thing to say and she rounded on him angrily. "All very well for you to talk! What about my animals! . . . What's going to happen to them? . . . What am I going to *do*?"

Halfway through his breakfast cereal, Jennings put

down his spoon and said, "I must go up and see Emma at once, Auntie. I've just had an idea."

"I hope it's better than the one you had yesterday," Angela said drily.

Her nephew ignored the rebuke. "I've been racking my brains all night. Tossing and turning, trying to think of something. I don't suppose I had a single wink of sleep all night long."

He had been fast asleep when she had looked into the spare bedroom shortly after saying goodnight, but she refrained from comment. Instead, she said, "Finish your breakfast first, anyway. And for goodness sake be careful. I don't want any more neighbours complaining to Mr Fagg."

Sub-Officer Sparrow had already left for the fire station and his wife, a nursing sister at the local hospital, was asleep after a tour of night duty when Jennings arrived at the flat.

Emma, waif-like and woebegone, let him in and they conferred in whispers in the hall.

"It's hopeless – quite hopeless," she lamented after warning him to keep his voice down as her mother was in bed. "I lay awake all night wondering what to do – well, *part* of the night, anyway," she amended.

Jennings sympathised briefly with his fellow-sufferer from insomnia, but he could hardly wait to explain his latest plan.

"Now, listen. We know it's no good trying to find homes for them in the flats because everybody comes under the same rule," he began. "But if we offered

73

them to a pet shop, they'd be bound to take them, wouldn't they!"

"Would they?" Emma sounded doubtful.

"Well, of course. They'd jump at it. Especially if we said they could have them free of charge: it'd be good business for them, too, because they could sell them to good homes and make a profit, and the animals would all be properly looked after."

The idea seemed feasible. Emma cheered up considerably. Indeed, the more she thought about it the more sensible it seemed to enlist the support of a pet-fancier whose animal-loving customers lived in homes where the borough housing department's regulations did not apply.

"Come on, then," she said. "There's a pet shop in Spencer Road. Let's go and see if they'll take them."

It was the first really hot day of the holidays. The sun beat down from a clear blue sky and the dusty pavements shimmered in the morning heat.

Spencer Road, when they got there, turned out to be one of the dozens of dingy side streets leading off the main thoroughfare. Emma led the way at a rapid trot past small shops selling paint brushes and hard-board and filling stations advertising car-washes and cut-price batteries.

"It's somewhere along here. We went past it in the car one day," Emma said as they panted along in the hot July sun. "I've never been in, though. I always get my pet food at the supermarket."

Jennings slackened his pace to a walk and said, "No

need to run all the way. I shall melt if I go any faster. How about an ice-cream?"

"Business before pleasure," Emma retorted. "You can eat all the ice-cream you want on the way back."

At that moment they came in sight of the place they were looking for, a small, single-fronted lock-up shop with no name on the fascia board and steamed-up windows.

"Perhaps it's better inside," Emma said hopefully as her companion pushed open the door.

But it wasn't better inside. The air was stifling and the smell of caged animals was overpowering.

Jennings pulled a face and wrinkled his nose. "Phew! You expect a bit of a pong in a pet shop, but this knocks you sideways."

There was no one to serve them so they were free to look round; and they were not impressed with what they saw.

There were tiny bird cages which gave the occupants little room to hop about; there were terrapins crawling over one another for lack of space; fish gasped for oxygen at the surface of their tank. There was a white mouse, dead in the corner of an over-crowded cage.

Jennings and Emma were appalled. "I'm not leaving my pets in a dirty little dump like this," Emma protested. "We'll have to find somewhere else, John."

"Come on, then; let's go now, before someone comes to serve us," Jennings urged.

At the door he turned to find that Emma was not following. Instead, she had gone across to the shop window where a large, white rabbit had attracted her attention. She exclaimed in dismay, removed the animal from its hutch and turned back with it cradled in her arms.

"Just look at this!" she cried indignantly. "He was lying all flopped out on his side and gasping. He'll be dead in two bats of an eyelid if he's left baking in that window. You just put your head in there. It's like an oven!"

The rabbit lay in her arms, its eyes staring and it sides heaving. It was no wonder that it had been overcome by the heat, for the cage had been left in the direct rays of the sun: there was no vestige of shade behind the glass and the atmosphere was suffocating.

The creature's fur was hot to the touch when Jennings put out a hand and felt it. "He's in a pretty bad way. We ought to tell the shop people," he decided.

There was a door leading to a back room behind the counter, and as there was still no sign of a shop assistant Jennings went up to the door and knocked loudly on the panels. "Shop!" he called. "Anybody there? . . . Sho-op!"

In the distance they heard a door bang.

"About time somebody turned up," stormed Emma, fanning the rabbit and looking round in vain for a shady corner in which to put it down. "Leaving animals in a blazing hot window with the sun beating down! I'll have something to say to whoever—"

She broke off as the inner door was flung back on its hinges and a spotty, pale-faced youth in a stained T-shirt and faded jeans came catapulting into the shop. Jennings had to leap aside to avoid a collision.

"What's all this, then? What's going on? Bomb going off or something?" the spotty youth demanded in a high-pitched, nasal voice.

"I was just trying to make somebody hear," Jennings explained.

"No need to knock the door in. I was out the back, having a cup of tea." His beady eyes came to rest on Emma. "So you want to buy the rabbit, eh!"

"No, I don't want to *buy* him. I just want to—"

"What you got it out the window for, then?" the youth broke in. "You got no call to touch the stock, except when you're going to buy it."

Emma quailed slightly under his bullying tone and Jennings jumped in quickly. "We just thought we'd better tell you."

"Tell me what?"

"It's half dead. It's been stuck in the window in the blazing sun with no room to move. Can't you put it somewhere cooler?"

The assistant took a quick look at the rabbit and shrugged his shoulders. "Not my place to touch anything I don't work here regular," he said. "I'm just looking after the shop till the bloke comes back Friday."

"But the rabbit will be dead by then if he's left where he is."

"Have to take its chance then, won't it! It's no skin off my nose. I tell you, I don't work here regular." The youth put out his hand to take the rabbit and Emma shrank back clutching it to her chest.

"Surely you could do *something*," Jennings urged.

77

"You could pull the sunblind down for a start. That'd give him a bit of shade."

The youth shrugged again. "Can't do that. It's wedged. The bloke said not to touch nothing. 'No need to touch nothing', the bloke said. 'Just put out the food like I said. The stock will be all right till I get back'."

It was clear that he knew nothing and cared even less about the welfare of the pets left in his charge. Emma felt sick with frustration. What could they do? A feeling of helpless rage welled up inside her and she burst out. "You ought to be arrested for cruelty to animals. Look at them all – moping and drooping and only half alive."

The spotty assistant wasn't prepared to argue. "I've had enough of this," he said. "Coming in 'ere, telling me what to do. I know your sort." He advanced upon Emma, took the rabbit from her grasp and put it down on the counter. "Go on! Get out of here, the pair of you!"

As he stood scowling at them, the shop door opened and a plump, dowdy woman came in laden with plastic shopping bags full of groceries. The sight of an adult customer cooled the young man's temper to some extent, and in a slightly more restrained manner he went on, "Right, now, it's like I said. If you don't want to buy the rabbit, keep your thieving fingers off the stock."

"I'd buy him if I could, just to get him out of your clutches," Emma retorted. "But I couldn't, anyway, even if I had the money, because—"

"All right, then, clear off, or I'll put you out myself."

"Don't you talk to her like that," Jennings said angrily. "We're not going to let the rabbit die just because you're too lazy to do anything about it. You ought to be reported."

"That's right," said Emma. "You're not fit to look after living creatures."

"You heard what I said!" squawked the pimply youth. "Get out of here before I start in on the pair of you!"

By now they were all three shouting at the tops of their voices: the noise was considerable. Suddenly, the woman with the shopping bags thundered, "Shut up, the lot of you!" in tones that set the tins of catfood rattling on the shelves.

The interruption shattered the clamour like a gun-shot, and the angry trio swung round in surprise. In the heat of the argument they had forgotten about the dowdy customer. Now she came forward shaking her head in disapproval.

"Shockin'! Never heard such a row! Worse than animals," she protested in a strong cockney accent. "What's all the shemozzle about, anyway?"

"It's this rabbit. He's going to die unless somebody rescues him from this man," Jennings told her. "It's like a bakehouse in the window and he won't even give him any shade."

"Not my place to interfere." The assistant was on the defensive now. "I don't work here regular."

The plump woman inspected the prostrate animal carefully, clucking and muttering to herself under her breath. "Tut – tut – tut . . . shockin' . . . disgraceful!"

Finally, she said, "Sooner we get it out of here the better." She turned to the spotty young man. "I'll buy the rabbit. It's not worth much, seein' the state it's in."

At the prospect of a sale the assistant did his best to sound obliging. "It's a bit skinny, perhaps," he conceded. "Soon fatten him up and get a bit of meat on him, eh!"

"Fatten him up! Meat on him!" The customer's tone was scathing. "What's this, then – a pet store or a butcher's shop! I'm buying the poor beast because I'm sorry for it – not for my Sunday dinner!"

She produced her purse from the depths of a shopping bag and made the purchase without further comment. Then she picked up the rabbit and thrust it into Emma's arms.

"There you are then, dear. He's yours now. Mind you look after him!"

Emma gaped at her. "Oh, but I don't want it. I mean – er – well, it's very kind of you, but I can't accept it – really I can't."

"Why not? You said you'd buy it if you had the money. I heard you tell the man."

"Yes, I know, but—"

"Well now I've bought it for you, so what are you grumbling about?"

Emma didn't know what to say. She was deeply grateful to the plump woman, but she knew that it would be asking for trouble to burden herself with yet another four-footed friend.

Seeing Emma floundering, Jennings hastened to explain. "We didn't know you were buying it for us,"

80

he pointed out. "We thought you were going to keep it yourself."

"Me, keep it! Are you being funny!" The stout customer picked up her shopping bags and waddled to the door. "No good expecting *me* to look after it, sonny boy. I live in a council flat, see. No pets allowed!"

Chapter 7

Change of Plan

It was shortly after midday when Aunt Angela drove back to Gaitskell Court to collect some documents she needed in connection with her work. As she walked from her car to the main entrance she met the caretaker emptying litter-bins in the courtyard.

He greeted her with a rueful smile. "You're asking for trouble walking about in the open with those neighbours of yours still on the warpath. They won't forget yesterday afternoon in a hurry."

Angela sighed. "I'm sorry they got so upset about it. The children went round to apologise last night, but they wouldn't listen."

"I'm not surprised. They're never happy unless they've got something to moan about." He shook his head sadly. "The kids will have to watch their step, too."

"They're doing their best," she told him. "They went out after breakfast to try and find a home for the animals. I hope they've been lucky."

"They'd *better* be lucky!" Mr Fagg replied with

feeling. "I've had enough of Emma Sparrow and her capers."

"Don't be too hard on her, Mr Fagg. I'm sure she won't do it again."

"She better hadn't! I tell you, Miss Birkinshaw – and this applies to your nephew, too – if I catch them trying to smuggle any more animals into these flats, I shall – I shall—"

His words died away and he stood staring before him in speechless amazement . . . Tip-toeing furtively round the corner of the building came Jennings and Emma, the latter clasping a large white rabbit in her arms.

Mr Fagg danced with frustration. "Cor! Stone the crows! They've gone and done it again!" he cried when the power of speech returned. "Just look at 'em Miss Birkinshaw. Can you believe it! In broad daylight too!"

Emma and Jennings stopped dead in their tracks on seeing the adults ahead. Then, realising that it was too late to retreat they advanced somewhat self-consciously to the main entrance.

"Good morning, Mr Fagg," Jennings said politely. "We – er— We were just – er—" He racked his brains for some nonchalant phrase. "We didn't expect to run into you, did we, Emma? It's – sort of – what you might call a coincidence."

"We thought you'd be indoors having your dinner," Emma added tactlessly.

"Stop trying to sound innocent, both of you," Aunt Angela said sternly. "What have you been up to now?"

While Emma and Jennings were pondering their

reply, Mr Fagg answered the question for them. "I'll tell you what they've been up to, Miss Birkinshaw. Wilful and deliberate flouting of the housing department's regulations." He wagged a large and toil-stained forefinger at the embarrassed culprits. "I gave you fair warning! I told you to get rid of those perishing animals, and instead of that you go out and get another one." He thumped the tarmac heavily with his broom handle. "Right! I'll be round the Town Hall first thing tomorrow morning to report this to the housing department."

"Oh, but please, really, you must listen," Emma implored. "We didn't want the rabbit, but we had to take him because the woman lives in a council flat."

"And where do *you* live – Buckingham Palace?" the caretaker demanded.

"No but, well, you see—"

At that moment a possible solution to their problems flooded into Jennings' mind. Of course! Why hadn't he thought of it before!

"Hey, listen, I've got an idea!" he broke in.

Emma gave him a withering look. "Not another pet shop, thank you. I'm off pet shops, just at the moment."

"No, it's nothing like that. I can't tell you any more yet, because I shall have to make arrangements, but I'm sure it'll be all right." He turned to the caretaker. "You said we could have till tomorrow night, Mr Fagg. They'll all be gone by then – even the rabbit. Honestly, I shan't let you down."

Mr Fagg pursed his lips and leant heavily on his

broom-handle. He seemed to be wrestling with a vital decision. Finally, he nodded a grudging assent.

"T't! The things I do for you kids!" he said in resigned tones. "You're more trouble to me than all my money!"

All the way up in the lift Jennings simmered with excitement. He refused to tell Emma about the plan he had in mind until he had made sure that it was workable; but as soon as Aunt Angela and he had reached the privacy of Flat 64, the details came flooding out in a wave of triumph.

"I must be mad! I can't think why I never thought of it before," he exclaimed, shooting himself in the head with an imaginary revolver. "That woman where we camped at Southcombe. She takes in animals that haven't got a home. I'm sure she'd have Emma's if we rang up and asked her."

It sounded a good idea. "Right then! What's her name and address?" asked Angela, reaching for the telephone.

The triumph in her nephew's eyes gave place to a look of stern concentration and he flicked his fingers to stir his sluggish memory. But it was no use.

"I can't remember," he said. "All I know is, she's a bit old and wears wellies and lives in a tumbledown sort of place with wobbly fences."

Angela put the telephone down. "I doubt whether Directory Inquiries will be able to help. They don't have lists of elderly women in wellingtons – not even in the Yellow Pages."

But, try as he would, Jennings couldn't bring her name to mind, so Angela rang the post office at Southcombe village stores where the postmistress (who knew everyone for miles around) suggested she should ring Mrs Hockin of *The Retreat*, and obligingly gave her the telephone number.

"That's the place," Jennings agreed. "I remember now. It's just come back to me."

Aunt Angela gave him a look and dialled the Southcombe number.

Mrs Hockin, talkative as ever, spent twenty minutes of expensive telephone time explaining that, although she was used to horses and had once been asked to take charge of a lion cub, she had never before been called upon to look after anything as small as a gerbil. However, she would be more than willing to take Emma's livestock into her care and felt sure they would be happy at *The Retreat*. "Tell the children to bring them down tomorrow. I shall be at home all day."

Jennings was delighted with the news and was impatient to rush up to Flat 72 to assure Emma that her problems were now over. He promised to come straight back, for it was now so near lunch time that Angela postponed her plans for going out again until after the meal.

When her nephew re-appeared some ten minutes later, she said, "I've thought of a snag, John. I shan't be able to take you in the car tomorrow. I'm booked up with appointments all day."

His face fell: for he had just learned from Emma that both her parents would be on duty the following day and would be unable to help with transporting the animals to their new quarters.

"Never mind," he said. "We can easily go by train."

The suggestion seemed practical. Southcombe was only twenty-five miles away on a direct rail route, and they would be able to catch a train at the local suburban station instead of having to set out from a London terminus.

So, with only slight misgivings, Aunt Angela agreed. After all, she reasoned, the children were old enough to undertake a straightforward journey by themselves; and the caretaker's deadline of Thursday evening for the pets' removal allowed no time to make other arrangements.

"You'd better tell Mr Fagg, John," she said.

"We've already arranged to," Jennings told her. "As soon as he comes back after his dinner. I bet he'll be pleased, don't you!"

However pleased Herbert Arthur Fagg may have felt at the news, his expression retained its usual gloom when Jennings and Emma raced up to him on the courtyard to announce the latest developments.

"H'm! How are you going to get them to Southcombe?" he wanted to know. "Build an ark, or fly them by helicopter?"

"We're going by train," said Emma.

Mr Fagg pursed his lips and looked doubtful. "First of all you've got to get them to the station," he said to Emma. "A right Charley you'll look, my girl, traipsing along the High Street with a hedgehog under one arm, a rabbit under the other, balancing a bowl of goldfish on your head with a tortoise trotting at your heels. And that's only *half* the menagerie!"

Mr Fagg had certainly raised a point. In the first flush of success in solving the main problem they had overlooked the question of embarkation.

"What we need is someone with a van. Some kind person just to run us to the station." A note of childlike innocence crept into Emma's voice and her gaze, sweeping the courtyard, came to rest on the caretaker's mini-van parked in a far corner. "Let's think, now. There must be *somebody* we know who's got a little van."

Mr Fagg could see which way the conversation was drifting. "Don't look at me like that, young Emma," he said defensively. "I'm a busy man."

"Oh, I wasn't thinking of asking *you*, Mr Fagg," the girl answered, wide-eyed with bogus surprise. "I didn't mean *your* little van – even though it's just what we need, and we don't know anyone else who's got one, do we, John?"

Jennings played up admirably. "We can't ask Mr Fagg, though," he said solemnly.

The caretaker heaved a sigh of mock resignation. "T't! You can't win with kids, can you! Twist me round their little fingers, these kids do!" he said, addressing his remarks to a nearby litter-bin. "I'm too soft – that's my trouble."

"You mean you'll take us?" cried Emma.

"Only to the station, mind," he said hurriedly. "And take that surprised look off your face: it doesn't fool me."

"Oh, thank you, Mr Fagg. Thank you very much indeed!"

Mr Fagg shook his head sadly. "The things I do for these kids," he grumbled, appealing to the litter-bin for mute sympathy. "There must be easier ways of earning a living!"

Considering that they were sharing the compartment with a hedgehog, a kitten, a white rabbit, a tortoise, a playful puppy and two gerbils, Emma and Jennings had a reasonably trouble-free journey to Southcombe on Thursday afternoon. Apart from the black-and-white mongrel, Ben (who, at a guess, was about three months old), the animals were confined in cardboard cartons and spent the time in snoozing or nibbling the assorted lunch-packs which Emma had provided for their refreshment.

The goldfish were not amongst those present. Jennings had conceived the bright idea of releasing them in an ornamental lily pond in a local park where they had swum off contentedly to join others of their species. "They'll be better off there: they like company," he assured Emma.

When the train reached Southcombe the cartons were gently lifted off the racks and deposited on the platform. Emma held the frisking Ben on a lead while Jennings looked about him, trying to get his bearings. He had passed by the railway station when returning to camp with Mr Carter; but, seen from the platform, the view looked unfamiliar and he wasn't sure which way to go.

The porter who collected their tickets was helpful. "Turn left outside the station," he told them. A thought struck him and he added, "It's a tidy step, though. You're not aiming to carry those boxes all the way to *The Retreat*, are you?"

"We shall have to. We haven't got any transport," Jennings explained.

The porter whistled in surprise. "You'll be down on your benders before you're halfway! You'd best leave them here with me till you've had a word with Mrs Hockin. She'll be ready enough to pop down for them in her car later on."

They were more than grateful. The prospect of carrying the cartons as well as leading the dog had been haunting them ever since they got on the train.

"There's a short cut to Mrs Hockin's about half a mile down the road," the porter went on. "Not easy to find though, because it's all wired up."

"Yes, I remember it," said Jennings, recalling the route the campers had taken along the right-of-way. "I don't want to run into old Major What's-his-name again, though."

The porter bristled with righteous sympathy. "Don't you be put off by *him*, son! He's got no right to stop you using that path. Local people walked it for years before he came here, throwing his weight about."

Emma grinned. "It doesn't sound as though he's a friend of yours."

"No more he is!" The porter's tone was scornful. "I like birds, see! I like watching 'em; it's my hobby, as you might say." He pushed his cap to the back of

"Are you aiming to carry those boxes all the way to The Retreat?" *asked the porter*

his head and prepared to expound his views on the shortcomings of the unpopular landowner. "Now Major Rudkin, he shoots bullfinches in case they eat his blackcurrants. I call that disgraceful – daft, too! I mean, you can sit and watch a bullfinch for hours on end, but you can't sit watching a blackcurrant." He snorted. "Well, you *can*, of course, but you'd need your head seeing to."

After some minutes they managed to steer the conversation away from the major's anti-social behaviour and, with Ben tethered to Emma's wrist, they set off down the road.

It was easy enough to find the stile when they reached it, but not at all easy to climb over it to gain the footpath.

"I reckon we'll need wire-cutters," said Emma, but her companion found a gap and held up the wire while she crawled beneath. He lifted the dog over the barrier, then scrambled through himself and led the way along what remained of the path. Quite soon there was no path to follow and they trudged on in what Jennings hoped was the general direction of Mrs Hockin's property.

All the time he was alert for any sight or sound of the major; but all was quiet and as they pressed forward his bump of geography seemed to improve and he recognised landmarks which convinced him that they were going the right way.

"I think we're nearly there," he said at length. "I've just seen the hole that old Darbishire fell into."

"Who?"

"Darbishire. Friend of mine. He was on the look-out for cannibals when we were coming along here, only he's a bit short-sighted and he fell into an elephant trap by mistake."

Emma laughed, and turned to admonish the dog. "Stop pulling, Ben you stupid animal. You'll have us both in an elephant trap if you go on tugging like that."

The advice was wasted on Ben. For the first time in his short life he found himself in a world of nose-twitching smells, and surrounded by a jungle of bracken which any right-minded dog would naturally want to explore. It was frustrating, being kept on a lead in this canine paradise, and with every new smell that floated past his nostrils he tugged and bounded, almost jerking Emma off her feet.

Now, as she tried to drag him past a rabbit hole, the puppy resisted, planting all four paws firmly in the soil and straining backwards with all his strength. The tug-o'-war was shortlived, for the next moment the dog's collar was jerked forward over his head, Emma collapsed backwards and the puppy was free.

Emma got to her feet, laughing. "I'll have to tighten his collar," she said. "Come on, boy, back on the lead! You can't run about where you like, here."

But Ben had other ideas. Far from responding to the call, he darted off into the undergrowth yapping excitedly.

"Hey, quick, get him!" Jennings cried, bounding into the bracken in pursuit and calling the dog. Emma followed, and for some minutes they tracked the puppy's progress by the sound of the high-pitched barking. Then the sound grew fainter as Ben ran further into the distance and the only guide to his whereabouts was the occasional waving of a clump of ferns as the animal ferreted in the undergrowth.

"This is frantic," moaned Jennings, coming to a stop and gazing round helplessly. "How are we going to get him back?"

Emma shrugged. "Just have to wait till he comes."

"Yes, but will he *ever* come back? He's not trained: he doesn't know where he is. He may just run off and get lost."

They stood still, shouting the dog's name and whistling; although this, in itself, caused Jennings some anxiety, for he had no wish to draw attention to the fact that the dog was out of control on private property.

"We'd better split up. You go over there towards the trees and I'll search the other way towards Mrs Hockin's," he decided after some minutes of calling had produced no result. So off they went, whistling, listening and scanning the undergrowth.

The searchers were a hundred yards apart and out of sight of each other when the yapping broke out again – a succession of frenzied yelps suggesting that the dog was hot on the trail of a rabbit or a squirrel. The commotion was coming from a spot nearer to Jennings than to Emma, and at once he started running in the direction of the sound.

As he did so, a shot rang out from a clump of bushes behind a clearing some distance ahead. Jennings stopped dead in his tracks, his heart thumping, while from behind him Emma shouted in alarm, "John, John!

Somebody shooting!" (an unnecessary warning in the circumstances) and at that moment the gun barked out a second time.

"He'll hit Ben. Stop him, John, quick!" Emma yelled, crashing her way through the undergrowth towards her companion.

Jennings was tense with apprehension. It was unlikely that the unseen marksman was deliberately aiming at the dog, but Ben's unpredictable behaviour might well take him into the line of fire. Leaving Emma to follow, Jennings rushed towards the bushes from which the shots had rung out.

"Stop, stop!" he called as he ran. "Please put your gun down. You'll kill our dog – he's somewhere in the bracken. For goodness sake don't shoot."

The bushes parted and a shortish, red-faced man in tweeds with a gun under his arm came out in the clearing.

"Come here, boy!" said Major Rudkin. "I want a word with you."

Chapter 8

Mrs Hockin's Dilemma

Jennings approached the major warily. He was still quivering with agitation: the shooting had come as a shock for which he had been unprepared. In a voice that was not quite steady, he blurted out, "You were shooting at our dog!"

The landowner dismissed the accusation with a snort of contempt. "As it happened, I wasn't even aiming at the brute; though I should have been justified in doing so, in the circumstances. Any dog running loose over my property does so at its peril." His eyes were hard and there was menace in his voice. "And the same applies to trespassers. You know this wood is private?"

"I've seen the notices – yes," Jennings agreed. "But there's a public footpath going across."

"That's beside the point. You're not *on* the footpath. And neither is your dog."

Emma arrived then, panting from her chase through the undergrowth. Fear for Ben's safety had driven all other considerations from her mind. "We're looking for our dog," she gasped out. "You scared him with your gun."

The major glanced without interest at her and said shortly, "Get off my land, the pair of you. Get back to the road at once."

"We can't go without the dog," Jennings argued. "When we've found him we'll go back as far as the footpath – but that's all."

Major Rudkin glowered. "I'm not prepared to argue. Anyone caught trespassing on my property with dogs out of control—"

"But we're not trespassing," Emma broke in. "We're going to see Mrs Hockin, and this is the shortest way to her house. The porter told us at the station. I'm sorry about the dog, really I am, but he won't do any harm. He's only a puppy and I'll put him on the lead as soon as we find him."

"*If* we can find him, after all that shooting," Jennings muttered. "He may be miles away by now."

It was not often that the major encountered obstinate trespassers who argued with his decisions. "I've had enough of this nonsense," he said angrily. "If you kids aren't back on the road in two minutes I shall—"

He broke off as a high-pitched "Coo-eee! Hullo there!" sounded from beyond the bushes a short distance away. All three swung round at the interruption which was followed some seconds later by the sight of Mrs Hockin making her way towards them through the undergrowth. Cradled in her arms was Ben, contentedly nibbling her fingers.

"Thought I heard voices," she boomed as she strode up to join the group. She nodded briefly to her neighbour. " 'Afternoon, Major. Hope you haven't been

97

disturbed by this – er – this little invasion of your territory. I'd have met the children at the station if I'd known what time they were coming."

Jennings and Emma sighed with relief at Mrs Hockin's timely arrival. Now, at least, they had a grown-up on their side to act as their spokesman.

"So you're John!" Mrs Hockin went on, smiling at Jennings. "I remember you now. I couldn't put a face to you when your aunt rang up. All you young campers looked alike to me." She transferred her smile to Emma. "And you're the young villain who's been breaking the rules about keeping pets, eh!"

Emma grinned, happy again at the sight of the puppy in the newcomer's arms. "Thank goodness you've found Ben. I was worried stiff when he ran off." She replaced the collar round the dog's neck and made sure it was tight enough to resist any further attempts to escape.

"He's perfectly all right now. It was probably the shooting that upset him," Mrs Hockin replied, handing the puppy back to its owner. "I found him tearing round my paddock so I guessed that you two weren't far away."

They must be quite close to *The Retreat* for their voices to have reached the ears of Mrs Hockin, Jennings reasoned. He was pleased to think that his bump of geography had, after all, been leading them in the right direction.

All this time Major Rudkin had been standing in frowning silence, stroking the barrel of his gun. Now, he said, "It's time we got this straight, Mrs Hockin.

98

Heaven knows I've been patient enough in the past about your animals breaking through into my wood; but I am *not* going to allow your guests to exercise their wretched little dog on my land."

"Oh, but it wasn't like that at all," Emma said quickly. "You see, what happened was—"

Mrs Hockin stopped her with a raised finger. "Yes, dear, I know what you're going to say, but I'd rather you didn't butt in, if you don't mind. This is just a little matter between Major Rudkin and me, and I'd rather handle it myself."

Emma looked contrite. "Oh, I'm sorry. I didn't mean—" she stammered.

"I suggest you both take the dog back to *The Retreat* and wait for me in the paddock," Mrs Hockin went on, pointing the way beyond the bushes. "I'll be with you in a minute or two."

Jennings and Emma were only too pleased to part company with the irascible major and set off at once through the bushes. Emma tied the dog's lead to her wrist. She was taking no chances.

When they were out of earshot Mrs Hockin turned to her neighbour. "Well, really, Major, I do think you might have shown a little more tolerance, considering the children had a perfect right to use the footpath. The very idea of scaring them off with a shotgun!"

"I did nothing of the sort. I was shooting rabbits," the major defended himself. "And their wretched dog completely ruined my sport, chasing about out of control and barking."

"Maybe so, but you can't blame the children for

99

thinking you were trying to hit him. I will *not* have my guests bullied in this way."

For some moments they stood glowering at each other, the man smouldering with anger and the woman defiantly determined to maintain her rights. At length the major said, "Mrs Hockin, you force me to speak plainly about this so-called animal refuge of yours. To my way of thinking it's an absolute menace. In the past few weeks I've had your donkeys, your goats, your dogs and goodness knows what else straying on to my property."

This was undeniable. "Well, I'm sorry, but it's only rough woodland. You can't claim that they do any damage," she replied with an edge on her voice.

"They might do a great deal of damage," he insisted. "They might disturb my partridges."

The rearing of game-birds was an issue on which the neighbours held very different views. "Poor birds, I'm sorry for them," said Mrs Hockin. "I look after my animals because they're in need. You look after your partridges so that you can shoot them."

It was not a tactful remark and the major bridled indignantly. He wasn't going to let this woman speak to him like that and get away with it. He'd show her who held the whip hand! However, he controlled his rising temper and said in matter-of-fact tones, "I would remind you that you are obliged by law to maintain a stockproof fence on the boundary of your property."

This, too, was a fact that could not be gainsaid, and Mrs Hockin knew she was skating on thin ice when she tried to belittle the accusation. "I admit the fence is tumbling down in a few places. I'll do what I can to get it repaired."

"I'm not asking for it to be *repaired*." The major's tone was icy. "I insist upon it being completely replaced."

She stared at him with mounting concern. She couldn't possibly afford to buy hundreds of yards of stockproof wire fencing. "That's rather a tall order, isn't it!" she faltered.

A smile twitched the corners of Major Rudkin's mouth. He knew she couldn't afford the outlay involved and was counting on the fact to bring her to heel.

"That's the position," he said in satisfied tones. "So long as you keep any form of livestock on your land I have the legal right to insist that the entire boundary is made proof against straying animals. Failure to do so will result in my taking action against you in a court of law. And you know what the result of *that* will be!"

At once the sparkle went out of her eyes and she suddenly looked haggard and pale. She had always known, deep down, that the major had it in his power to bring her welfare work to an end on the grounds that her animals constituted a nuisance; but she had never allowed herself to be daunted by what in the past had seemed no more than a vague threat. Now, it seemed, the threat was becoming a reality.

Slowly the colour came back to her face and she said in a low voice, "Yes, Major Rudkin. I know only too well what the result would be if you took me to court."

Emma and Jennings had spent a fascinating ten

minutes in and around the paddock and stables making friends with a motley rag-bag of dumb friends. Jennings, having met most of them some days earlier, was very much at home when introducing them to Emma who, for her part, was delighted to have found such a comfortable haven for her pets.

"I shall pay Mrs Hockin for their keep, of course. That's only fair," she said as they rounded the corner of the stables. "I'll have a word with her about it when she's finished talking to that ghastly gunman."

In the distance they could see their hostess coming slowly over the paddock towards them. Her walk had lost its usual springy gait and as she drew near they could see the worried frown on her brow.

"Are you all right, Mrs Hockin?" Jennings asked.

She recovered her poise and laughed. "Silly me, silly me, silly me!" she said, shaking her head. "Opening my mouth too wide as usual, and putting my big foot in it."

Emma nodded her sympathy. "Major Rudkin, I suppose?"

"Who else! He's just delivered his ultimatum. He's within his legal rights, of course, but if he takes me to court I shan't have a leg to stand on."

Emma and Jennings looked at each other in bewilderment. Why should he want to take her to court?

"The animals, dear," she explained. "They have a tiresome habit of wandering where they will and ignoring the major's boundaries. So he now insists that I put up a brand-new stockproof fence." She gave a hopeless shrug.

"Financially, of course, it just isn't on: the stuff costs a fortune. Goodness knows how much it would take to fence the whole length of the boundary."

Jennings said unexpectedly, "I'll work it out for you."

Ignoring Emma's look of incredulity, he furrowed his brow in concentration. Not knowing the price or the length required, he would have to work it out by algebra . . . H'm! Well, supposing the fencing cost – say – x pounds per foot, and the distance to be covered was – well, call it – y hundred feet. That meant that the total cost to the nearest pound would be . . . H'm! Let's see now.

"It would cost you xy hundred pounds," he announced proudly.

Emma pulled a derisive face at him. "Hark at ye computerised think-tank," she said. "*Anybody* could work it out like that. What's it *really* going to cost?"

"I'd need a little more data to work that out," Jennings said with dignity.

Mrs Hockin laughed. "And I'd need a little more money to pay for it. I certainly haven't got xy hundred pounds in my piggy-bank. There's only one answer to the problem, so far as I can see," she went on as she lead the way towards the house, "and that's to get rid of the animals."

Emma was appalled at the thought. "Oh, *no*! You couldn't do that."

"I may have to. No straying animals – no need for a stockproof fence. It's as simple as that."

"But it's not fair," Emma burst out, her eyes flashing

with anger. "You're doing a wonderful job here and – and—" She broke off, her feelings too deep for coherent speech.

They were crossing the stable yard when a further disturbing thought occurred to Mrs Hockin. She laid her hand on the girl's shoulder and said, "About Ben, dear. I'll do my best to keep him, of course, but if all the animals have to go that may include him, as well."

Emma seemed to crumple at the news. Her face fell and she stared at her hostess in dismay. Having just brought the puppy to a good home in ideal surroundings, the prospect of having to find another one was more than she could cope with. Mrs Hockin noticed her distress and said, "Of course it may not come to that; but he's not trained, you see, and the major's bound to make trouble if he wanders over the boundary."

"Yes, I see that," Emma said miserably. "It's not your fault, Mrs Hockin."

There would be no problem about housing the "small fry" as Mrs Hockin termed the rest of Emma's menagerie. They, unlike Ben, would be content to settle down in their new quarters with no ambitions to explore the surrounding countryside.

"What have you done with the rest of the tribe?" Mrs Hockin asked as they went into the house.

They told her about the bird-watching porter and she nodded approvingly. "They'll be safe enough with him. Jack Hobden's a great chap with animals. They say in the village that he'll keep a train waiting in the station rather than disturb a baby rabbit on the line."

They had a substantial tea in the kitchen and spent some time settling the dog down in its new quarters. Emma was heartbroken when the time came to say goodbye to Ben, but Mrs Hockin's open invitation to come and visit the animals whenever she could, cheered her up to some extent.

After that, they had a bumpy ride to the station in their hostess's dilapidated car. The vehicle was twelve years old, and the bodywork was so decayed in places that the passengers had to be careful not to poke their feet through weak spots in the floor.

Mrs Hockin seemed to have banished her financial worries to the back of her mind, for she kept up a flow of light-hearted chatter as the car chugged slowly along the road. But Jennings, seated in the back, found himself pondering the major's threat. Could he really obtain a court order to close the sanctuary if the animals weren't properly fenced in? Presently he said, "Look here, Mrs Hockin, how would it be if Emma and I tried to raise some money to help you buy your new fences?"

Mrs Hockin laughed, and the car swerved slightly as she turned her head towards the back seat.

"Very kind of you to suggest it, my dear," she said when the vehicle was again under control. "But unless you happen to win a football pool or something, I doubt whether it would add up to very much. I shall count up my pennies and do what I can but, frankly, I'm not hopeful."

By now they were in sight of the station where the porter was waiting with the five cardboard cartons of small livestock. Jennings loaded the car while Emma gave Mrs Hockin strict instructions about nursing a convalescent hedgehog back to health on an invalid diet.

It was time, then, for Jennings and Emma to cross to the far platform to catch their London train. At the top of the steps they turned and waved goodbye.

"I meant what I said, Mrs Hockin," Jennings called down from the footbridge. "I reckon, between us, we ought to be able to scuttle old Major Trigger-Happy. Just you wait!"

Chapter 9

Boxing Clever – Sitting Pretty

All the way back in the train, Jennings and Emma discussed the threat that was hanging over the animal sanctuary. It was unthinkable that Mrs Hockin should be forced to abandon her good work – there must be *something* they could do to help her to pay for the new fencing.

Jennings, proud of his reputation as a deviser of ingenious schemes, was unwilling to admit that he had no ready answer to the fund-raising problems; and they were nearing the end of the journey when he said, "Mind you, I've got lots of brilliant ideas, really, but the trouble is I shan't be here to carry them out. My Mum and Dad will be back from Norway next week."

Emma smiled at him mockingly. All this talk of brilliant ideas was mere bluff. "Name one," she challenged. "I'm listening."

Jennings wasn't prepared to be as definite as all that. "Well, like, say, for instance, delivering newspapers."

107

"Fine, if you can get taken on. There just aren't any paper-rounds going begging in our part of the world."

"Well, baby-minding, then."

She shrugged. "Hopeless! It'd take forty years to buy one post, let alone *y* hundred yards of fencing."

"All right, then – you suggest something."

But Emma's ideas were no better than his, and as the train was now drawing into the station they had to postpone their deliberations.

When Jennings arrived back at the flat, Aunt Angela greeted him with the news that his mother had telephoned from Oslo during the afternoon. "They're coming back on Monday so we can go and meet them at the airport," she told him.

Jennings was delighted. He had not seen his parents since the previous half-term and could hardly wait to tell them all the things he had been doing in recent weeks. All the same, this meant that he would have to hurry his bright ideas along if he was to think of any money-raising suggestions before he went home.

Next morning after breakfast he went upstairs to Emma's flat to discuss a vague plan that had been running through his mind ever since he had woken up. The door was opened by Mrs Sparrow whom he had first met the previous day when Emma and he were getting the animals ready for their journey.

Jane Sparrow was a friendly woman in her late thirties who with her slim build, large brown eyes and wide mouth bore an uncanny resemblance to her daughter. Indeed, at their first meeting Jennings had been so struck by the family likeness that he had been unable to resist switching his gaze from one to the other, marvelling at the similarity.

"I guessed it was you ringing the bell, John. The furniture's still vibrating," she said as she let him in. "Emma's in the living room; she swears she's doing her piano practice, but you can't believe everything you hear, can you!"

When the pianist emerged, Jennings outlined the plan he had in mind. He felt diffident in putting it forward for it was not one of his best ideas, but it was all he'd been able to think of.

"What I thought was, how would it be if we held something like, say, a sort of bazaar-thing. You know, selling home-made cakes and home-grown lettuces and stuff."

He had been expecting Emma to pour scorn on the suggestion, but to his surprise she seized on the idea readily.

"Yes, why not!" she agreed. "We could have it out-side in the courtyard. And as it's in aid of animals we could call it the Animal Fair." She danced round the hall singing:

> "All the birds and the beasts were there
> By the light of the moon the big baboon
> Was combing his auburn hair."

"Don't get too excited. I'm going home on Monday," Jennings said, bringing the song-and-dance act to an abrupt halt.

"As soon as that!" She refused to be daunted.

"You'll have to get your skates on then, won't you, if you're going to help." For some moments she frowned in thought. "We couldn't do this by ourselves though – just the two of us – even if we wanted to. We'll have to rope in neighbours and people."

"Such as who? Mrs Pratt and Mrs Plumrose?"

Emma laughed and threw a cushion at him. "Look, I know millions of girls in the flats – well, a few, anyway. Let's go and round some of them up and see who's willing to help."

They spent half the morning calling at various flats, explaining their plans and enlisting support. To begin with, the response was lukewarm – apart from Mrs Sparrow and Aunt Angela who both agreed that the idea was worth pursuing. So many people were away on holiday that their plans did not really begin to take shape until they sought out two girls in Emma's year at school who lived in an adjacent block.

The first of these was Maggie, a red-headed, serious-minded girl of twelve with musical interests and a talent for playing the clarinet. She it was who had found the injured hedgehog in the Surrey lane and had passed it on to Emma for its period of convalescence. The second hopeful choice was Cleo, a West Indian from Trinidad with an irresponsible sparkle in her eyes and a happy knack of laughing her way through most of the problems of life. Both girls had known about Emma's secret menagerie and both were keen to help now that the need had arisen.

Emma formed a committee on the spot and the four

of them went back to her flat to plan out ways and means.

"Right! I declare this meeting well and truly open," Emma announced to the committee seated on the floor. "The first thing to decide is how we're going to get people to rally round and make things to sell."

Maggie, the self-appointed hon. sec., made a note of the chairman's opening remarks.

"We'll want a stall for home-made things like hand-knitted bedjackets and baby clothes, and another for home-grown produce like rhubarb and stuff."

"I just *love* hand-knitted rhubarb," Cleo murmured.

Emma gave her a look. "Ha-ha! Very funny . . . And then we'll have a white elephant stall with mammoth bargains and—"

"Are we going to sell mammoths as well as elephants?" Cleo inquired with wide-eyed innocence.

"Somebody will have to gag that girl, or I shall resign," the chairman threatened.

Despite interruptions from Cleo, the overall pattern of the Animal Fair began to emerge after twenty minutes of brain-searching and discussion. If all went well they would have a stall for cakes and various foodstuffs, another for new and secondhand clothing, and a white elephant stall at which they would offer anything from priceless antiques to useless junk which they could persuade neighbours and well-wishers to part with.

Then there were the fairground attractions to be considered. There would be a raffle, of course – that would be easy to arrange: and Maggie was keen to organise a game of skill which she had seen at a church bazaar, some weeks earlier. The apparatus was complicated to describe and nobody could follow the details, beyond grasping that the game was something to do with rolling ping-pong balls down a drainpipe and catching them in a jam jar.

"All right, we'll do that then, if Maggie knows how to fix it up," Emma decided. "It should bring in quite a bit if we charge 10p a go with a bar of chocolate for the winners." She wrinkled her nose in thought. "Another thing we could have is a competition for guessing the weight of a cake, if we can find someone to make us a really big one."

Maggie said, "They say Mrs Plumrose is a good cook."

Emma cowered in mock terror. "You do the asking then! She's still got John and me in her gunsights over what happened at Miss Birkinshaw's last Tuesday."

Cleo rocked with laughter. "If she won't make us a cake we could get people to guess the weight of Mrs Plumrose, instead. Twenty-three stone in her bedroom slippers, I'd say."

Soon they had enough suggestions; more than enough really, for they were aiming to do most of the work themselves and each new proposal meant finding more volunteers to swell the ranks of the helpers. Moreover, Jennings' impending departure on Monday meant that he would be unable to help with the preparations, but he assured them he would do his best to come back for the day in three weeks' time when the fair was scheduled to take place.

"Well, that seems to have got most of the problems buttoned up," said Maggie, running her eye down the list of activities. "We'll have to do a door-to-door canvas through the block telling people all about it, and getting them to—" She paused and scratched her nose thoughtfully with her pencil. "There's just one thing, though: we haven't got permission to hold this fair yet, have we?"

Nobody had thought of that.

"I didn't think we needed to," said Emma. "After all, we live here. It's our courtyard, so who's going to stop us?"

Maggie said, "Mrs Pratt, for one. She lives here, too, don't forget, and she's bound to kick up a fuss. Probably get round old Fagg to ban it. After all," she went on, doodling a caricature of Mrs Pratt on her list of activities – "after all, if the housing department can stop you keeping pets, they can stop you turning the courtyard into a sort of Battersea Funfair if they want to."

Maggie had certainly raised a point and for some moments they sat pondering this threat to their plans. Then Jennings said, "I reckon we'll get permission if we ask properly. I'll go and see old Fagg. I've got a feeling he's on our side, on the quiet."

Emma cheered up at once. "I'll come with you, then. And while we're working on him, you two can start chatting up the neighbours. The more people we can get to support us, the better."

It was late afternoon before Jennings and Emma were able to find the caretaker. They had been watching out for him on the courtyard but he didn't appear, so eventually they extended their search and came across him on the fourth floor landing trying to clear a blocked rubbish-chute with a drain-rod.

He listened to their request with pursed lips and gloomy head-shakings.

"It's no good asking *me* for permission. I'm only the caretaker: I haven't got the authority," he told them. "You'd have to go round to the housing department and talk to the manager."

"OK, we'll do that, then," Emma agreed readily. "What d'you think he'll say?"

Mr Fagg's gravelly voice churned out an impersonation of the official in question. "He'll say, 'Run away, little girl, can't you see I'm busy? I've got enough to do without you kids coming round bothering me'."

Jennings was stung by this example of adult injustice. "But that's not fair! We're doing this for a good cause. He'd *have* to listen to us."

"Don't you believe it! The manager won't want to get involved in case some of the residents start raising objections. There's one or two round here who think you kids get your own way too much, as it is."

"So you think there's no point in asking?"

"Hopeless, I'd say. Just a waste of time." He turned back to the rubbish-chute and went on poking with his drain-rod.

Emma and Jennings looked at each other in quiet despair. They were utterly deflated: their plan had collapsed before it had had a chance to get off the ground.

Jennings said in a resigned voice, "That's it, then! If

it's a dead duck, we'll have to call the whole thing off. Thanks for telling us, anyway, Mr Fagg."

He turned and led the way back to the stairhead, Emma following with a dejected droop of the shoulders. But before they had reached the half-landing, they heard the caretaker calling them. Puzzled, they went back up the stairs to see what he wanted.

"I've been thinking," he said. "Who's going to be the guest of honour to declare this fair of yours open?"

It was a surprising question considering what he had been saying a few moments earlier.

"Nobody. It's all off," replied Jennings. "You just said yourself it was hopeless."

"I said it was hopeless for *you* to go to the housing department – or me either, come to that." Though his voice remained gloomy there was a flicker of interest in Mr Fagg's eye which seemed to confirm Jennings' hunch that the caretaker might well be a secret ally. "So if you kids want this caper of yours to go ahead, you'll have to start acting a bit crafty."

They stared at him blankly. What on earth was the man talking about? Seeing their bewilderment, he went on, "Now supposing you got somebody like the lady mayor to open this money-raising lark for you—"

"Lady mayor!" Emma echoed in amazement. "You must be joking. She'd never come!"

For the first time the caretaker's features creased in a slow smile. "I wouldn't bet on that," he said. "Our friend Alderman Mrs Freeman is always going on about the lack of community life on the housing estate. OK,

115

then, here's your chance to show her you want to do something about it."

The name of Alderman Freeman meant nothing to Jennings, though Emma had seen her on mayoral visits to her school and had once presented her with a bouquet of flowers at a prize-giving ceremony. To the grown-ups of the borough, however, Mrs Freeman was a local legend – a well-loved figure who worked with tireless devotion for the community in which she lived.

Emma was overcome with shyness at the thought of approaching such a celebrity with such a trivial request, but Mr Fagg dismissed her fears with a wave of his drain-rod.

"Nonsense! I know Connie Freeman – known her all her life," he confided with a chuckle. "She's not the sort who likes mayoral pomp and all that gobbledegook. She likes ordinary people, like you and me."

It was left to Jennings to point out what seemed to be a serious flaw in Mr Fagg's argument. "That's all very well," he said. "But what's the use of asking the mayor to open the Fair if the housing department say we can't have one?"

Mr Fagg permitted himself the luxury of another throaty chuckle. "Ah! Well, that's where we start boxing clever," he said, his husky voice rasping like a spadeful of clinker in a cement-mixer. "This is where we kill two birds with one stone, as you might say. You kids go and call on Alderman Freeman: tell her what you're aiming to do, in a good cause. That'll get her on your side, if you play your cards right."

"Yes, but I still don't see—"

"And if she agrees it's a good idea, you go and tell her about the trouble you're having in getting permission. Pass the buck to her, as you might say. She'll soon put the housing manager in his place."

Mr Fagg's plan was becoming clearer and Jennings, in particular, was most impressed. As one who spent much of his free time at school in devising schemes to outwit the authorities, he felt that here was a plan to which he could give his approval. Mr Fagg – a man after his own heart – showed promise as a hatcher of plots: the idea of using the mayor to do the donkey-work for them was, in Jennings' opinion, a most ingenious piece of conspiracy-making.

"You're sure she'll be able to persuade the housing people to let us have it?" he queried.

"Well, if *she* can't, then nobody else can," Mr Fagg retorted. "The housing manager just about drops down on his benders whenever he meets the mayor. Once you get Connie Freeman backing you up, you're sitting pretty."

Emma skipped with joy and tugged at Jennings' elbow. "Come on, then, John; let's go round to the Town Hall and see if we can see her." Still skipping, she started off along the landing, but Mr Fagg, waving his drain-rod like a magician's wand, stopped her dead in her tracks.

"Don't you do that! Don't you go round the Town Hall, young Emma Sparrow," he said severely. He drew in his breath sharply to show his disapproval. "Tut-tut-tut! Ruin the whole plan, that would!"

"But surely, you just said we ought to—"

"Ah, but how about if the mayor isn't there and you run into the housing manager instead! You'd have shot your bolt and got nowhere." Mr Fagg slammed shut the door of the rubbish-chute and wagged a filthy forefinger at his fellow-conspirators. "Now listen! You've got to box clever on this one. You go round to her house and see her privately. Get her hooked on the idea before these Town Hall busybodies can get at her." He lowered his voice and winked. "Try and catch her first thing tomorrow morning before she starts her day's work."

It was sound advice and they decided to act on it, so after thanking the caretaker for his words of wisdom, Emma and Jennings took the lift up to Aunt Angela's flat to look up the mayor's address in the telephone book.

"I had a feeling that Mr Fagg was on our side, on the quiet," Jennings said, flicking through the pages of the directory. "Fancy him coming up with a wheeze like that!"

"And telling us how to go about it, too!"

Jennings grinned. Doing his best to imitate the caretaker's deep, gravelly voice, he rumbled, "If you want to end up sitting pretty, young Emma Sparrow, you've got to start off boxing clever!"

Mrs Ada Plumrose stood at her front door on Saturday morning listening with a closed mind to the two girls on her doorstep. She preferred talking to listening and, though Cleo and Maggie had been explaining their mission for five minutes, it was clear from the blank look on her face that her brain cells had failed to process the data.

"No, I wouldn't want nothing like that. I don't hold with it," she was saying in her dull, flat voice. "I support the housing department. No pets allowed, and quite right, too."

Maggie stifled a sigh of exasperation. "You don't understand, Mrs Plumrose. It's nothing to do with allowing pets in the flats. This bazaar we're getting up is to raise money for an animal welfare project, out in the country."

A trace of understanding glimmered in Mrs Plumrose's eye and she sniffed with disapproval.

"We've never had nothing like that round here, before. Always been a respectable block, this has," she said. "I don't want nothing to do with that sort of thing."

A front door slammed across the landing and Mrs Pratt came out of her flat carrying a pink plastic shopping bag. At once, Mrs Plumrose's face lit up with neighbourly interest.

"Ah! There's Mrs Pratt going out," she observed chattily, and called across the landing, " 'Morning, Mrs Pratt. Going shopping, are you!"

Her neighbour turned back from pressing the lift button. "What did you say, Mrs Plumrose?"

"Going out, are you?"

"No, I'm going shopping."

Seeing the two girls on the doorstep, Mrs Pratt abandoned the lift and came across to join in the argument.

She, too, had received a visit from Cleo and Maggie earlier in the morning.

"Have these girls been on to you about this thing they're on about?" she demanded.

Mrs Plumrose nodded. "They've just been telling me. I don't want nothing to do with it."

"No more do I," Mrs Pratt agreed. "I wouldn't give it house room."

"It won't need house room," Cleo said sweetly. "We're holding it out of doors."

"Tut! Making cakes and knitting bed-jackets – the very idea," Mrs Pratt went on disgustedly. "I wouldn't have the time – not with five nights a week Bingo."

There was no point, Maggie decided, in continuing the pointless discussion. She turned away saying, "That's all right. You needn't help if you don't want to. We just thought we'd ask."

At that moment the lift door swung open and Emma and Jennings stepped out, having learned that their friends were at work on level five. They were both looking remarkably pleased with themselves.

"Good morning!" Emma called cheerfully to Mesdames Pratt and Plumrose. "Has Maggie been roping you in to help?"

"Not me, she hasn't," Mrs Plumrose said firmly. "I don't hold with it."

"That's a pity. We were going to ask you to bake us a cake."

Mrs Plumrose was outraged. "Well, I like your sauce!" she protested.

"But if you'd rather do something else, that'll be all right with us, won't it, John?"

Jennings, beaming in the background, came forward and said, "Yes, of course. For instance, we shall need someone to present a bouquet to the mayor when she declares the fair open." Ignoring the gasps of incredulity which greeted this announcement, he hurried on, "And then there's that competition about rolling ping-pong balls down a drainpipe. You might like to help with that, instead."

The two women were staring at him in disbelief. "What's that you said?" demanded Mrs Pratt.

"Rolling ping-pong balls down a drainpipe."

"No, no, no! About the mayor. *She's* not coming to this do of yours, is she!"

"Yes, of course. Emma and I have just been round to her house to ask her, and she said she'd love to. She's very keen on people getting together and working in a good cause: she told us so!"

There was a short, stupefied silence while the news sank in. The fact that the mayor had pledged her support placed the matter in a new light. It was natural enough for Mrs Pratt and Mrs Plumrose to disapprove of a project sponsored by schoolchildren: but Alderman Connie Freeman, JP, was a very different kettle of fish!"

"The lady mayor!" Mrs Plumrose breathed in an awed whisper. "I should never have believed it." Already she was planning which dress to wear for the occasion: while her neighbour — also looking ahead — could see in her mind's eye some lines in the local paper which ran: *The mayor was conducted round the stalls by Mrs Prudence Pratt of 33 Gaitskell Court.*

"Still, if you don't want to help, we won't waste your time telling you about it," Jennings threw in non-chalantly.

This wasn't at all what the ladies wanted. The moment had come to express their approval – not too eagerly, of course: after what they had been saying, there must be a slight show of reluctance.

"Mind you, looking at it one way, it *is* a good cause, isn't it!" Mrs Pratt conceded. "I mean – animals and all that."

And Mrs Plumrose added, "Well, I suppose I *could* just find time to make a cake. Seeing the mayor is coming, it wouldn't seem right *not* to, somehow."

So that was settled! Having thanked the good ladies for their co-operation, Jennings and the three girls went off in the lift to hold a meeting in Emma's flat.

For some moments after the committee had gone, Mrs Pratt and Mrs Plumrose stood on the landing discussing the unexpected development. Mrs Pratt, starry-eyed at the prospect, gave a self-conscious giggle and said, "Name in the paper! Fancy that! I've always wanted to see my name in the paper. Perhaps a photo, even, as well!"

Not to be outdone, Mrs Plumrose said, "I've had my name in the paper before now. When my chimney caught fire over in Balham. It said, 'Mrs A. Plumrose, thirty-seven, in brackets, of 54 Church Road—' "

"Thirty-seven!" her neighbour echoed incredulously.

"That's what it said," Mrs Plumrose maintained. She

wasn't going to admit that the reporter had got her age mixed up with the number of her house. A thought occurred to her and she added, "Here, I'm going to have a sort-through of all that junk in my spare bedroom. There's bound to be something there that'd do for their white elephant, or whatever they call it."

Chapter 10

The Fun of the Fair

Jennings was overjoyed to see his parents at the airport on Monday. There was so much to talk about, starting as far back as half-term when the family had last been together.

Anxious though he was to listen, Jennings was even more eager to talk, which meant that his parents' account of their travels became mixed up with his own account of all that had been happening to him.

Even before they had left the airport, Mum and Dad had to hear about the time when Darbishire dropped his plimsoll down a manhole; about Venables absent-mindedly coming down to breakfast in his pyjama jacket instead of his shirt; about Temple sitting on an ants' nest at a school picnic. On the way home they heard about Mr Carter's new camera and Mr Wilkins' prowess at camp cookery and, of course, about Emma Sparrow's secret menagerie and recent events at Gaitskell Court. Indeed it was several days before Jennings had talked himself to a standstill and all members of the household had been brought up-to-date with family news and views.

The next two weeks passed all too quickly, packed with the ingredients of a busy holiday at home: and after that it was only a few days to the Animal Fair and time for Jennings to think of going back to Gaitskell Court. It was an easy journey by rail and, as his mother was otherwise engaged for the afternoon he was happy enough to go by himself. He arrived at the flats shortly before two o'clock to find that Emma and her friends had not been idle during his absence.

The courtyard was humming with activity. Half a dozen trestle tables had been set out on the tarmac stacked with a variety of home-made foodstuffs, pot-plants, baby-linen and household goods. Beyond these were the fund-raising competitions and games of skill designed to entice the patrons to dig down into their pockets. Young helpers whom Jennings had not seen before were putting the finishing touches to the stalls and attractions.

A slim figure in oriental dress with a yashmak over her face accosted him as he stood looking around the unfamiliar scene.

"Greetings, stranger! You come to consult Madame Cleopatra, mystic visionary of the Orient?"

"I beg your pardon?" said Jennings, taken aback.

The mystic visionary hooted with laughter and slipped the veil from her face.

"Oh, sorry, Cleo, I didn't recognise you," he said, joining in her laughter.

"Just as well you didn't. That's the whole point of the disguise," Cleo explained. "If the neighbours find out that Madame Cleopatra is really that noisy girl

125

from Flat 39 they won't want to dish out 50p to have their fortunes told."

Maggie hurried into view carrying a bunch of slightly withered geraniums. She grinned at Jennings and said, "We forgot about the bouquet for the mayor so I've had to pick these instead. Don't tell old Fagg. He'll go mad if he finds out I've been raiding ye municipal flower-bed." She turned to Cleo. "We've had to scrub that idea about giving you a tent to do your stuff in. We couldn't get the tent pegs into the concrete, so you'll have to use that little shed where Mr Fagg keeps the spare dustbins."

"Dustbins! Charming!" said the oriental mystic. "Roll up and have your fortunes told in the caretaker's rubbish dump!"

"It's all right; he's swept it out. And put that yash-mak back over your face. You look better that way." Maggie trotted off to collect her book of raffle tickets and Jennings made his way across the courtyard, keeping an eye open for Emma.

First, he came across Mr Fagg muttering to himself with frustration as he sought to erect a flimsy contraption of hardboard, plastic drainpipes and jam jars. He greeted Jennings in martyred tones, "So you've come back now all the work's done! Wish *I'd* had the sense to keep out of the way." He jerked a derisory thumb at the ball-rolling gadget that was causing him so much trouble. "Tut! The things I do for you kids! On my day off, too!"

Emma was delighted to see Jennings again when he

126

found her arranging articles on the white elephant stall. "Come and see what we've collected," she said.

He ran his eye over the objects on the table: lamp shades, a copper kettle, two clocks, table-mats, a rusty toffee tin—

"That's not for sale: that's for putting the money in," she explained.

He continued his inspection: records, teapots, vases. Puzzled, he picked up a striped woollen object of indescribable shape. "What's this – a bagpipe cover or an octopus's football jersey?"

"Don't be cheeky!" She stifled her mirth with a frown of mock respect. "Mrs Pratt knitted that specially. It's a hot-water bottle cover."

"I beg its pardon," Jennings said humbly.

"She said she'd got something else for us, but she hasn't turned up with it yet." Emma swung round to the trestle table behind her where her mother and Aunt Angela were getting ready to serve cups of tea.

"Hey, Mum, I reckon we're a bit short of stock for the white elephant," she announced. "How about if I had another scrounge through the spare bedroom cupboard to see if there's any more stuff?"

Mrs Sparrow was doubtful. "You can if you like, but I shouldn't think there's anything left that's any good . . . And don't go mad," she called after her, as her daughter scurried away on her errand. "I don't want to go home afterwards to find the flat's been stripped."

Helped by her nephew, Angela lifted the tea urn on to the table. "I think we're about ready now," she said to Mrs Sparrow. "Apart from that cake Mrs Plumrose said she'd make for us. I hope she hasn't forgotten."

Mrs Plumrose hadn't forgotten. As Emma hurried in through the side door of the block, Mrs Plumrose and Mrs Pratt emerged from the main entrance dressed in their best and bearing gifts. Mrs Pratt was carrying a transistor radio which hadn't emitted a sound for some years. She would never have dreamed of giving it away, had it been in working order.

Mrs Plumrose's contribution was the cake for the weight-guessing competition. Knowing that the contestants would be expected to judge the weight by eye and would not be allowed to handle it, she had inserted the 2lb weight from her kitchen scales into the cake-mix before putting it in the oven. It was, she thought, a foolproof way of making sure that nobody was likely to win the prize.

The two ladies crossed the courtyard to the refreshment stall. "Here you are then, Miss Birkinshaw," said Mrs Plumrose, holding out her weighty contribution. There was no room among the tea cups to put it down, so Mr Fagg who had finished tinkering with his drainpipes took the cake while Angela cleared a space.

The caretaker's expression changed as he felt the weight. "Cor, stone the crows! What have we got inside this, then – cannon balls?"

Angela was shocked by this show of disrespect. "Well, really, Mr Fagg! It looks a lovely cake. Almost too good to eat."

"Oh, it's not for eating. It's for guessing the weight of," Mrs Plumrose explained.

"T't! Never mind about guessing the weight! How about putting the shot!" Mr Fagg set the cake down heavily beside the tea-urn while Angela hurriedly switched the conversation to a safer topic.

"And Mrs Pratt! Are you really giving us this lovely radio? It's too kind of you!"

"That's all right," said Mrs Pratt. "It doesn't work."

"Oh!"

"It *looks* all right, though, doesn't it! Makes a nice ornament, I thought."

"Er – yes, of course! Delightful!" Angela handed the gift to her nephew. "You'd better put it in the white elephant department, John. I expect *somebody* will be pleased to have it."

People were gathering on the courtyard awaiting the arrival of the mayor. The word went round that the local press car had been sighted, so Mrs Pratt and Mrs Plumrose hurried off in search of the reporter. If he had brought a photographer with him they would need to be in the front row when Alderman Mrs Freeman stepped out of the mayoral car.

Emma was back at the white elephant stall when Jennings strolled across with the transistor. Her search through the bedroom wardrobe had revealed a swim-suit and a pair of ballet shoes which she had grown out of: she had also found an old leather handbag which she hoped might sell for about a pound. They were adding the new stock to the pile when Maggie arrived in a state of panic.

"Hey, Emma, what am I supposed to be raffling?" she cried, waving the book of raffle tickets in the air.

"You can't expect people to fork out money for a ticket until they know what the prize is!"

Emma pulled a face. "We haven't got a prize. At least not yet. We'll have to think of something."

"Yes, but *what*? It's got to be something worth winning." Maggie ran her eye over the motley collection spread out on the trestle table. "None of this tatty old stuff's any good. Honestly, Em, what sort of a Charley d'you think I'll look trying to flog tickets at 20p a time when I don't even know what I'm flogging them for!"

The problem had to be shelved for the moment because Emma's mother came rushing up to announce that the mayor's car was turning in through the gates.

"Quick, quick! Off you go, all of you," she ordered, giving the girls a helpful push in the right direction. "You're supposed to be at the gate to meet her."

"Not me," said Jennings. "I missed out on all the hard work."

"Nonsense! It was you who suggested having a Fair in the first place. Off you go with the girls!"

Mrs Sparrow chivvied the little group across the tarmac to thread their way through the crowd gathering round the official car.

Mr Fagg watched them go, shaking his head and tut-tutting about the lack of security arrangements. Fancy going off and leaving the stall unguarded! Asking for trouble, that was, with goodness knows how many light-fingered strangers in the crowd looking for a chance to make a quick snaffle. *T't!* The girls would look a bit silly if they came back to find all the best

THE FUN OF THE FAIR

stuff had been pinched! He supposed he'd have to go and mount guard. *T't!* On his day off, too!

He strolled over to the trestle table where the old leather handbag took his eye. He looked inside. *T't!* Some mothers do have 'em, he thought. Just like a bunch of kids to leave a thing like this lying about.

In the distance the mayor was declaring the fair open: odd phrases from her speech floated across the courtyard. ". . . young people willing to show a bit of enterprise . . . let's make sure that their efforts are worthwhile . . . the tinkle of coins dropping into the toffee tins . . ." And more in the same vein. It was a good rousing speech interspersed with cheering and clapping from the crowd.

Mr Fagg nodded in approval as he picked up the broken transistor radio and opened the back. Then his expression changed. *T't!* Cor! Some people were so stupid they'd let their heads fall off if they weren't screwed on! . . . He fumbled in his pocket for his pen-knife, and got to work.

When the opening ceremony was over and the mayor was being shown round the stalls, Mrs Pratt and Mrs Plumrose made their way towards the spare dustbin shed.

"Now's your chance, then, Mrs Pratt, if you want your fortune told," her neighbour encouraged her. "There's that Madame What's-it, look, standing in the doorway. They say she comes from the East. You can tell she's foreign, what with those robes and that cloth over her face."

"Yashmak," corrected Mrs Pratt.

"Eh?"

"That thing she's wearing. They call it a yashmak."

"Who does?"

"Foreigners out East. It's so you can't see her face."

"Well, of course you can't! Not with that cloth over it," Mrs Plumrose retorted. "I don't need foreigners out East to tell me that."

Cleo, on the lookout for customers, advanced to meet them. "Greetings, ladies! You come to consult Madame Cleopatra, mystic visionary of the Orient?"

"Oh, I say," simpered Mrs Pratt.

"I foretell the future. All secrets are revealed to me through my occult powers." The bogus accent was a mixture of Pakistani, Chinese and Welsh. "You cross my palm with silver coin!"

Mrs Pratt fumbled for silver in her handbag. "Oh dear, I don't seem to have the right change."

"That's OK by me," said Cleo, her accent slipping into Camberwell cockney. "I'll take 50p in coppers, if you like." She curtseyed and led the way into the spare dustbin shed.

Mrs Plumrose was enjoying a cup of tea at Angela's refreshment table when her neighbour re-joined her ten minutes later.

"Oh, it was lovely," Mrs Pratt reported, starry-eyed with excitement. "They read the future like a book, these orientals. She told me things about myself you wouldn't credit!"

"Fancy that, now," marvelled Mrs Plumrose.

"She knew I went to Bingo five nights a week. She even knew which Sunday papers I took."

"*I* could have told you that," her neighbour pointed out.

"Ah, but *you* don't come from the East. *She* does! And that wasn't all. She told me about a dark, bearded stranger and said I was going to get a lovely surprise before the day was over. How about that, then!"

It occurred to Aunt Angela that Mrs Pratt was taking the fortune-telling prophecies rather too seriously. "You mustn't really believe what she told you," she said. "It's only meant to be a joke."

"Joke!" Mrs Pratt rounded on her sharply. "What d'you mean – a joke?"

"Just a bit of fun. She's not *really* a fortune-teller from the East. She's Cleo Markham, the girl from Flat 39."

"She never is!"

"Oh, yes. Didn't you guess? We thought it would be a good way of adding to the fun of the fair. We never expected people to believe it."

As the truth dawned, Mrs Pratt's starry-eyed rapture changed to glassy-eyed consternation.

"So that's the game! A proper fool I've been made to look," she blazed indignantly. "I'm going to give that young madam a piece of my mind."

"Oh, please don't say anything," Angela entreated. "The girls were only trying to entertain you."

"You may call it that, Miss Birkinshaw, but I know better. I've been insulted, that's the long and short of it."

Desperate, Angela thrust a fifty pence piece at the

dissatisfied client. "Here, I'll give you your money back."

But it was no use. Mrs Pratt, nursing her grievance, made off to the spare dustbin shed thirsting for revenge. Mrs Plumrose went along too, anxious not to miss what looked like being a first-class row.

Angela sighed as she watched them waddling away over the tarmac. "Why did I have to go and open my big mouth?" she asked herself.

Chapter 11

Mr Fagg Mounts Guard

Shortly after the mayor had finished her tour of inspection, Jennings made his way back to the white elephant stall. Emma was already there, still arguing with Maggie about the raffle.

"It's no good asking *me* what the prize is," Emma was saying. "I told you I forgot all about it. Terribly sorry."

"Sorry! I should hope so. We'll have to scrub the raffle, that's all. And after I went to the expense of buying all these books of tickets." Maggie, flouncing away in a huff, stopped in surprise as a sudden blare of pop music rang out from the far end of the stall. Turning, she saw Mr Fagg twiddling the knobs of Mrs Pratt's transistor.

"Here you are then! How about this for the raffle," he called after her. "You couldn't want a better prize than a radio in perfect working order. Cost you pounds to buy one like it."

Emma was delighted. "Oh Mr Fagg, you've got it going."

"Didn't need much to put it right. Just a few wires

come adrift, that's all." He thrust the set into Maggie's hand. "Here you are, girl. Don't stand there listening to this unmusical tripe. Get on and sell some tickets."

Mr Fagg had gone back to take charge of the ball-rolling competition when Mrs Sparrow stopped by the white elephant stall some while later. Business had been brisk to start with and by now most of the best bargains had been sold.

"It was a good job I got those extra things from the spare bedroom," Emma remarked to her mother. "We've sold the lot."

Mrs Sparrow ran her eye over the sparsely-stocked table. "I only hope you were careful what you took."

"Of course I was: just things like my old swim-suit and those ballet shoes. And that old brown handbag that you never use."

A look of alarm flashed in her mother's eyes. "Not the *leather* handbag."

"Yes, why not! It was tucked away behind our winter coats." Emma laughed. "It wasn't much good, though. I only got eighty pence for it."

Emma's laughter stalled as she caught sight of her mother's expression. "What's up, Mum? What have I done? It was only an old bag and it was empty."

Mrs Sparrow seemed to age ten years in ten seconds. "Emma, you little idiot!" she said sadly. "It was *not* empty."

"It was. I looked, Mum – honestly."

"Yes, but not in the lining, child! You didn't look in the lining!"

Emma shook her head. She'd been in too much of a hurry to bother about anything like that.

In a low voice Mrs Sparrow said, "There was £230 tucked away in the lining of that bag. I've been putting away a fiver a week since last summer for our holiday."

The little group round the table stared at her in dismay, and Emma burst into a flood of tears. "Oh, Mum! I never knew, Mum. I never knew."

Though deeply distressed, Mrs Sparrow put a brave face on things. "Of course you didn't know, love. It was going to be a surprise." She shrugged. "If only I'd known what you were doing! Still, it's a bit late to say that now."

Jennings was aghast at the news. He swung round to the tear-stained culprit and cried, "Who did you sell it to, Emma? Can you remember?"

Emma pulled herself together with an effort. "Yes, it was a woman in a yellow sweater. I'd never seen her before. I'm pretty sure she doesn't live anywhere round here."

"If she's still going round the Fair we may be able to find her," Jennings said, grabbing Emma by the wrist. "Come on, quick!"

For just a moment his companion wavered, too upset to move. Then she braced herself and followed.

"Come on," Jennings said again, leading her into the crowd. "Look for anyone in a yellow sweater. It may be hopeless, but we've got to do *something*."

There was a queue of customers waiting to have their fortunes told when Mrs Pratt stormed up to the spare

137

dustbin shed with Mrs Plumrose panting along behind her. Unable to jump the queue, and unwilling to join on the end, the two ladies were obliged to postpone their protest and went off to see what other attractions the fair had to offer.

To their surprise, they quite enjoyed themselves. Mrs Plumrose got quite excited about rolling ping-pong balls down a drainpipe and won twenty pence for her skill. And Mrs Pratt not only won a tin of beans at the hoop-la stall, but was snapped by the press photographer while doing so. She was so overcome with pride and confusion that shortly afterwards she bought a raffle ticket without thinking to ask what the prize was to be. By the time they had worked their way back to the dustbin shed, the queue had dispersed and the field was clear for Mrs Pratt to give Cleo a piece of her mind.

"You ought to be ashamed of yourself, my girl!" she began. "Pretending to tell fortunes and you only living in the next block, an' all. Disgraceful, I call it; don't you, Mrs Plumrose!"

"Shocking!" her neighbour agreed. "Dressing up like that with a cloth over your face. Never ought to be allowed!"

Cleo did her best to defend herself. "But it's all part of the fun of the fair. I thought you'd get a good laugh out of it."

"Huh! You don't catch *me* laughing!" And it was obvious from the tight set of her mouth that Mrs Pratt's sense of humour drew the line at such outrageous goings-on. "All those lies you told me about a dark, bearded stranger bringing me fame and glamour. What have you got to say about that?"

Cleo racked her brains for a plausible answer. Her eyes flashed with inspiration and she said, "How about the press photographer you were talking to! Supposing he puts your name in the local paper as a helper."

"I don't see what that's got to do with—"

"But of course! There's fame for you, Mrs Pratt! Glamour, too, if the photo comes out all right."

Surprisingly, Cleo found herself being backed up by Mrs Plumrose. "She's right, you know, Mrs Pratt. You always wanted your picture in the *Gazette*. Dark young man with a beard he was, too – just like she told you."

For a moment Mrs Pratt wavered. Looking at it one way, of course, the prophecy had come true, even though it fell far short of her expectations. On the other hand, she was surely entitled to something better than that for her fifty pence!

"Huh! Stretching it a bit, I'd say," she retorted, rallying to the attack. "And anyway, if she's so clever, what's this surprise she says she's got lined up for me?"

This time Cleo had no ready answer. Seeing her blank look, Mrs Pratt cried, "There you are! What did I tell you? It's nothing but a bare-faced swindle."

Just then, Maggie came hurrying round the corner of the dustbin shed and skidded to a halt beside her.

"Mrs Pratt, I've got news for you," she announced. "You've won the raffle."

Immediately, Cleo and her innocent deceptions were forgotten in this new excitement.

"Me! Really! Well, that's nice, I must say," Mrs Pratt exclaimed with satisfaction.

"Always lucky with the raffle, Mrs Pratt is," her neighbour observed enviously. "What's the prize, then?"

"A transistor radio."

"That'll be handy," said the lucky winner. "Just what I need, seeing as my old one—"

She broke off as she caught sight of the object that Maggie was holding out for her acceptance. "Hey, what's the idea! I'm not having *that* for my prize. It's my old one I gave to the white elephant."

"And now you've won it back again," Maggie returned coaxingly. "Lucky old you!"

Speechless with indignation, Mrs Pratt could do no more than point and gibber. When she could control her feelings, she said, "It's a swindle. That set's no good: it doesn't work. I shouldn't have given it away, else."

By way of reply Maggie turned a knob and at once the air was loud with the sound of music. "There you are, Mrs Pratt. It works like a dream now. It'll save you buying a new one."

This was undeniable and, once again, Mrs Pratt's mood took a turn for the better. "So it will," she agreed. "Well, this *is* a surprise, I must say."

"Surprise! Surprise!" echoed Cleo, standing behind her. "There you are, Mrs Pratt. The prophecy of Madame Cleopatra has come to pass. What d'you think of that!"

Mrs Pratt clearly didn't know *what* to think. Looking

slightly dazed she took the transistor without a word. Her neighbour, however, had something to say.

"The girl's right, you know, Mrs Pratt," she observed solemnly. "That's two things she told you come true. Can't begrudge her 50p for telling you that. Well, not seeing as how it's all in a good cause."

The music ceased as Mrs Pratt switched off the set. Perhaps she *was* being a bit unfair to the girl. After all, she reflected, it *was* a good cause, wasn't it – animals and all that!

There was a fair sprinkling of yellow sweaters on the courtyard, but none of the wearers bore any resemblance to the woman who had bought the old leather handbag. It was now mid-afternoon, all the best bargains had gone and people were beginning to drift away.

"I reckon she's pushed off – whoever she was," Jennings decided after their second tour of the courtyard. "We'd better try out in the street."

It was a hopeless quest. The crowds were dense in the High Street and when they tried their luck in the supermarkets they could hardly move against the throng of Saturday afternoon shoppers. It was like looking for a stick-insect in a thorn bush, Jennings thought, as they stood on the pavement scanning the bus queues and wondering what to do next.

"Better go back and tell your Mum," he decided. "If the woman's honest, of course, she'll take it to the police station – if she knows she's got it."

"If, *If*!" Emma echoed, her voice tense with

frustration. "Why should anybody even *think* of searching through the lining – unless they want to mend it."

Emma was becoming more and more edgy as the minutes ticked by. However understandable the disaster, it was an accident for which she alone must take the blame.

Low in spirit, they retraced their steps to Gaitskell Court and reported their failure to Mrs Sparrow.

"No luck, I'm afraid," Jennings greeted her when they got back to the white elephant stall. "We've been right down past the traffic lights and up as far as the Town Hall and there isn't a whisker of her anywhere."

Emma was in tears again. "Oh, Mum, it was all my stupid fault. And you'd worked so hard and saved up all that time."

"Never mind, love. Don't distress yourself," her mother comforted her. "These things happen."

"Yes, but it *needn't* have happened. The whole point of having this Fair was to *make* money: not for me to go giving it away to strangers. I feel terrible about it. I could—"

Her voice trailed to silence and she turned away racked with self-reproach as Mr Fagg plodded across the tarmac towards them. He stopped at the white elephant stall, noting Emma's obvious grief, and her mother's strained and worried look.

"Hullo-ullo-ullo, what's all this, then?" he demanded as cheerfully as his gravelly voice would permit. "We can't have tears on this festive occasion. Something wrong, is there?"

Jennings said gloomily, "Yes there is, but it's nothing

you can do anything about, Mr Fagg. Mrs Sparrow's lost some money."

The caretaker frowned and scratched his nose thoughtfully. "H'm! It wouldn't be a sum of £230 by any chance?"

"Yes, it would – it *is*!" Jennings cried with rising hope. "Why? How do you know?"

By way of reply the caretaker produced a bundle of notes from his trouser pocket. "Because that happens to be the exact amount I'm looking after until I find the rightful owner. It's all here, waiting to be claimed."

The shock was too much for Emma who started weeping again, but this time they were tears of relief.

Jennings was staring at the bundle of notes in puzzled wonder. "How did you get hold of it?" he wanted to know.

"Just used my loaf," the caretaker said simply. "You and Emma go trotting off to chat up the mayor, leaving me as guard dog." He sighed deeply, as a man weighed down by life's problems. "As though I hadn't got enough to do, what with chasing those perishing ping-pong balls all over the courtyard – and on my day off, too!"

"Yes, but what made you think of—?"

"Going through the handbag?" He laughed. "I went through everything, son – trust me! Only common sense, isn't it, when you're dealing with a scatter-brained bunch of kids like you lot."

There was no doubt about Mrs Sparrow's feelings as she took possession of her money. She said little, but the look of gratitude in her eyes said more than any speech of thanks. As for Emma, she flung her arms round Mr Fagg, causing him to back hastily and disentangle himself with every sign of alarm.

"Hey, you watch your step, young Emma Sparrow," he protested. "You'll be getting me talked about."

By now the crowd on the courtyard had gone and the helpers were beginning to pack up the trestle tables and take their jingling toffee tins to Aunt Angela who was acting as treasurer.

Cleo and Maggie strolled up to exchange fairground gossip. They were first appalled and then delighted to hear the saga of the old leather handbag.

"Any idea how much money we've made?" Maggie asked Emma.

"Not yet, we haven't. Miss Birkinshaw's still adding it up." Emma gave a little shiver of relief. "All I know is we're not starting off with a thumping great debt of £230 round our necks – thanks to Mr Fagg."

"Who won the cake-guessing comp?" asked Cleo, her yashmak dangling from her chin like a beard.

Jennings looked up from his job of bundling unsold articles into an empty carton. "We had to call if off – didn't you know? Mr Fagg accidentally dropped it on his toe and broke it."

"He broke his toe?"

"No, you idiot – the cake. Although he nearly ended up with a fractured toe, as well. Didn't you see him limping?"

Cleo's irreverent laughter startled the sparrows hopping round the refreshment table. "Some cake! I bet her puff pastry would go right through the floor-boards."

Jennings looked round to make sure that Mrs Plum-rose was not in earshot. "And I'll tell you another thing, but you'll never believe it," he went on. "When we picked up the pieces we found she'd left a 2lb weight inside."

"You're joking!" said Maggie. "What would she do a thing like that for?"

"There's only one answer to that," said Jennings. "She's either absent-minded, or shortsighted – or both."

It was, of course, the wrong answer: but none of the little group could think of a better one.

Chapter 12

Return to Linbury

It was some time before Jennings heard the financial result of the Animal Fair. He lost touch with Emma and her friends when he returned home on Saturday evening: and after that it seemed no time at all before the holidays were over and he was back at Linbury Court for the start of the Christmas term.

"Have a good holiday?" Darbishire greeted him when they met at tea on the first evening. Darbishire was suffering from a recent, very short haircut; and his new sweater – designed to allow room for growth – was ruckled in folds about his waist. His hands were lost in his sleeves which he had to keep pushing back above his wrists every time he took a forkful of sausage and mash.

"We didn't go away anywhere," Jennings told him. "Except to my aunt's and Mr Carter's camp, of course." His mind flashed back to the first week of the holidays. "Hey, you remember that Mrs Hockin person with all those homeless animals!"

Darbishire nodded. "And old Major Trigger-Happy and his shotgun."

"Well, I met her again in the holidays – and him, too. It was quite exciting really because—"

Jennings decided to begin at the beginning. Across the table, Venables, Temple and Atkinson pricked up their ears and joined the audience as Jennings related the story of Emma and her secret menagerie.

As they listened, the sausage and mash grew cold on their plates (except in the case of Temple for whom food was a serious matter). From their knowledge of the surroundings they could visualise Jennings' encounter with Major Rudkin: knowing Mrs Hockin, they could sympathise with her problem of replacing her fences. After that, they wanted to hear about the Animal Fair.

"How much money did you make?" Venables asked, returning to his congealing sausages.

"I don't know yet. Quite a lot, I expect. Perhaps over five hundred pounds," said Jennings, guessing wildly.

The wild guess came down to earth two days later when Aunt Angela wrote to tell him the result of the fund-raising effort. Jennings was bitterly disappointed. All that effort! All that hard work! (Not that *he'd* done much, but the girls had slaved like beavers); and here was Aunt Angela's letter reporting that the profit amounted to the measly sum of seventy-two pounds.

"Is that all!" said Atkinson when Jennings conveyed the news across the breakfast table. "You said you'd made five hundred pounds, at least."

Jennings pulled a long face. "Just shows how wrong

147

you can be. Talk about a slap in the face! Seventy-two pounds won't go far in helping to buy new fences."

Darbishire said, "It makes you mad, thinking of that old major getting the better of her. Why can't *we* do something to help?"

"Such as what?" demanded Venables above the crackle and pop of his detonating *Krunchie-Whispie* cornflakes.

"I don't know, but – well, she was really great to us in camp, wasn't she! If we could think of a wheeze to, say, double the money old Jen's girl friends managed to rake up, it might help a bit." Fired with enthusiasm, Darbishire went on, "Think how chuffed she'd be if some of us blokes who were at camp went trotting up to *The Retreat* with a massive great contribution."

"Contribution of *what*?" Venables persisted. "Purses of gold? Oil shares? Trading stamps?"

"No, but – well, *you* know." Darbishire shrugged and pulled his sleeves out of the marmalade. "There must be *some* way we could raise a spot of cash."

By bed time that evening, Jennings had thought of the answer.

"It came to me in a flash in the middle of Old Wilkie's geography lesson," he announced to Dormitory Four as they stood by the washbasins foaming at the mouth with pink toothpaste. 'It was old Darbi saying if only we could go *trotting* up to Mrs Hockin's that gave me the idea. How about a sponsored trot!"

"A sponsored *what*?"

"Trot. Like a sponsored walk, only faster. Call it a sponsored *jog* if you like, only it's quite a long way from

148

here to Southcombe – more than twenty-five miles, I should think – so we couldn't go flat out all the time."

"Twenty-five miles!" exclaimed Atkinson incredulously. "That's a *marathon*. You're off your rocker, Jen. *I* couldn't run all that way, and neither could you."

"You wouldn't have to," explained the creator of the bright idea. "We'd do it as a team relay. Say about six of us, running in pairs. When you and your partner had done, say, a couple of miles, the next two take over and you have a rest in somebody's car till it's your turn to go again. We shall be running against the clock."

Nods of approval greeted the explanation. The idea had possibilities. Provided that they could find enough sponsors at, for instance, five pence a mile, three pairs of runners might well be able to raise the £72 odd, needed to equal the sum collected at the Animal Fair.

The project would demand detailed planning, of course. The route to be followed and the mileage involved would have to be worked out. "And we shall have to get permish, too," Jennings reminded his – by now – enthusiastic listeners. "We'd have to do it on a Saturday and get the head to let a master come with us in the mini-bus."

Venables laughed. "Don't ask Old Wilkie to drive the bus. He'd go mad, crawling along all day at five miles an hour with a bunch of flaked-out jog-trotters in the back."

"How about refreshments?" queried Temple, anxious to get the priorities right. "I can't do more than two miles to the gallon on orange squash: and I'd need a few doughnuts to get me up the hills."

"All right, all right, it's early days yet," Jennings assured him. "The first thing to do is to get some expert advice and find out what the snags are."

There was no argument about where to seek expert advice. Mr Carter was the man they always turned to with problems too complicated for youthful minds to cope with.

Mr Carter thought it was a good idea when they went to see him about it at break next morning. He, himself, was a keen supporter of good causes and saw no reason why the animal sanctuary should not be chosen for a fund-raising project. And, indeed, from that time onwards the arrangements for the run were mainly in his hands.

He it was who persuaded the headmaster to release the runners from school on the third Saturday in October and to lend the school mini-bus for use as the team's back-up vehicle. He telephoned Mrs Hockin to make sure she would be at home when the runners arrived, and he alerted the school housekeeper to the need for suitable refreshment for the journey.

There were many matters to be considered, and Mr Carter made the boys work out the answers to some of the questions themselves.

"We're going to tackle some problems in practical mathematics this morning," he announced to Form Three a few days later. "I hope you've all got your wits about you because the running schedule for six members of this class is going to depend upon the answers that we come up with."

Form Three sat up, sharpened their wits and grinned at the six members concerned. In the front row Jennings, looking pleased and confident, grinned back; while Darbishire seated beside him assumed the modest expression of one who knew he was no athlete and reckoned himself lucky to have been chosen at all! Venables and Temple, the second pair of runners, frowned importantly to stress the serious nature of the enterprise; and in the back row Atkinson exchanged satisfied nods with Rumbelow, chosen by ballot to fill the last place in the team.

The first part of the lesson was spent in studying the Ordnance Survey maps provided by Mr Carter. The shortest distance by road was found to be twenty-two miles, but all agreed that it would be better to avoid main roads and plan a route along country lanes and footpaths.

Here were more problems: if the runners took to open country they would be out of touch with the mini-bus for long periods. Indeed, it soon became clear to the route-planners that the shortest distance from point *A* to point *B* was not necessarily the quickest or the best. In the end, they agreed that lanes wide enough for the mini-bus to follow would be a safer route than doubtful short cuts beset by hazards not clearly marked on the map.

"Pretty rough going, some of it, for a six-hour run," Mr Carter observed when the route was decided upon and the distance logged as twenty-four miles. "I suggest we aim at an average of a mile every fifteen minutes over the whole distance."

Rumbelow put up his hand. "I don't need a quarter of an hour to run a mile, sir. I could do it in less than half that time, easily."

"Maybe you could – when you first set off in the morning. It might be a different story by mid-afternoon, when you're climbing the North Downs. You'll have to keep strictly to the schedule, you know, or you'll find yourself in trouble."

The schedule looked easy enough on paper. Starting on the dot of 10 am the first pair of runners would set off while the rest followed in the van. At 10.30 – and thereafter at half-hourly intervals – another pair would take over the baton while the two breathless athletes would sit back in the vehicle recouping their energies for their next turn of duty. And so on throughout the day.

By four o'clock (and not a second later) the final pair must be knocking triumphantly at Mrs Hockin's door. If they failed, they would not be able to claim a single penny from their sponsors.

Atkinson blew out his cheeks and said, "Phew! Better not fail, then! I'm not going to run all that way for nothing."

"Ah, but what's the rate for the job?" queried Bromwich. "Supposing – only supposing, mind – I agreed to sponsor, say, Venables. What would it cost me?"

"One pound twenty: five pence a mile," replied the athlete in question.

"But that's crazy. *You* won't be running twenty-four miles – you'll only be running eight. The rest of the time you'll be sitting in the van with your great feet up."

"Let's get this straight," said Mr Carter. "You're not being asked to put your money on any single runner: the idea is to sponsor the team as a whole."

"Six runners for five pence! Pretty good value," Bromwich observed. "Especially with old Darbi in the team. He'll conk out after a few hundred yards, so it won't cost us anything at all."

"Very funny!" said Darbishire with lofty disdain: but at the back of his mind was a tinge of worry in case Bromwich was proved to be right.

The third Saturday in October was still nearly three weeks ahead: ample time, Jennings decided, to gather support and find enough sponsors.

The target was agreed at £72 – the same amount raised at the Animal Fair. "So if all six of us get ten blokes each at five pence a mile it'll work out just right," he told his team the day after the schedule had been prepared.

Venables looked impressed. "Did you just work that out in your head?"

"No. Mr Carter told me last night," Jennings admitted. "Sixty sponsors at one pound twenty pence a time: or if that's too much for anyone to fork out, he can rope in another bloke to go halves."

At first the sponsoring was slow, but it improved somewhat as it became known that well-wishers could guarantee a half, a quarter or even an eighth of the one pound twenty pence involved. Even so, they were still short of their target until one or two of the runners wrote to their parents to ask them to make up the deficit.

A week before the run they had the whole amount guaranteed, and Darbishire was jog-trotting round the playing field before breakfast each morning to improve his stamina. He even persuaded Mr Wilkins to come out on to the field to time him with a stop-watch.

It occurred to Jennings that Emma and her friends would be interested to hear of their plans: and though he normally rationed his letter-writing to one short epistle to his parents every Sunday, he managed to find time to scribble a note to No. 72 Gaitskell Court.

"Dear Emma, (he wrote).
I hope you are well and having weather. I expect you think what we made at the Animal Fair was a bit measly, considering. So what some of the blokes (plus me) are doing is a sponsored trot to Southcombe to get another contribution for Mrs H. It should go off all right if Darbishire (my best friend) doesn't snuff out on the way because he's not much good at running. We are going to do it like this . . ."

The letter rambled on, omitting most of the things that Emma wanted to hear about, but still containing enough information to fire her enthusiasm. At the family tea-table that evening she said, "John's doing a

154

sponsored run for Mrs Hockin. I reckon Cleo and Maggie and me and people ought to join in, too."

Mrs Sparrow read the letter. "They've obviously picked their team already. I can't see them inviting you to join the runners."

"Maybe not, but there's other things. We could get some more sponsors for them in the flats, couldn't we! Might even double the money they're hoping to raise."

"You could try," her mother agreed. "You'll have to find out more about it first, though. Nobody's going to sponsor a run until they know what they're letting themselves in for."

The details were supplied by Mr Carter when Aunt Angela telephoned him that evening. Armed with this information, Emma enlisted Maggie and Cleo in a door-to-door canvas of the flats to enrol further sponsors. Sometimes they were lucky; sometimes they met with a rebuff; and at other times (as in the case of Mrs Pratt and Mrs Plumrose) they had some difficulty in explaining what it was all about.

Cleo and Emma called at Flat 35 before leaving for school on Wednesday morning. Mrs Plumrose opened the door and stood listening to the girls with her mind elsewhere.

"What's all this, then? You trying to pull my leg, or something?" she said when Emma paused for breath. "The very idea – expecting me to run twenty-four miles."

"No, no, I didn't mean *you*, Mrs Plumrose," Emma said hastily; while Cleo bit her knuckles to stifle her mirth as a vision of Mrs Plumrose in track suit and running shoes flashed into her mind.

"I should think not, indeed! You don't catch me running – not on *my* legs. Not even when I see the bus coming. Wait for the next one, like any sensible person."

Emma tried again. "It's what they call a sponsored run, in aid of our animal welfare project. The boys are going to do the running at five pence a mile."

"What, on foot!" Mrs Plumrose looked surprised. "When I was a girl you could go by bus for less than five pence a mile. No point in running all that way when you can get a bus at the corner."

From the flat across the landing Mrs Pratt emerged with her pink plastic bag and was hailed by her neighbour with the usual greeting. " 'Morning, Mrs Pratt. Going shopping, are you?"

"What's that, Mrs Plumrose?"

"Going out, are you?"

"No, I'm going shopping."

Mrs Plumrose was anxious to discuss the latest news-bulletin. "What d'you think of the new dodge these girls have thought up, then? Going to run twenty-four miles for five pence."

Mrs Pratt had already heard about it. "Must want their heads seeing to," she said with a sniff. "Cost them more than that in shoe-leather."

"That's just what I was saying. Number 95 bus runs every ten minutes, weekdays. I'd go by bus if I was them."

"Not on Sundays, they couldn't." said Mrs Pratt. "Doesn't run Sundays."

"Ah, well that's it, then. No good if they aren't running, is it!"

Cleo shrugged helplessly and said, "I'm confused. Who's supposed to be running? The boys or the buses?"

It was time for the girls to set off for school, but, even so, Emma made a last attempt to explain the obligations of a "Five pence-a-mile" sponsor. When she had finished, Mrs Plumrose's face lit up with understanding.

"Oh, well if that's all you want, I suppose I might as well," she said. "Here you are, I'll give it to you now." Fumbling in her purse she produced a five pence piece which she solemnly handed to Emma.

Not to be outdone, Mrs Pratt passed a similar coin into Emma's hand. "After all, it's a good cause," she conceded. "I'm not against kindness to animals, don't think that. Only, don't take them on the bus with you on this trip of yours. Can't do that without the conductor's permission, you know."

Emma felt she was quietly going mad. But it wasn't worth going through the explanation all over again merely to point out that five pence represented only a twenty-fourth part of a sponsor's obligation.

So she smiled politely and set off towards the lift with Cleo by her side. As she pressed the lift button she shook her head and sighed.

"There must *be* easier ways of raising one pound twenty," she said with deep feeling.

Chapter 13

The Sponsored Trot

The third Saturday in October dawned with a hazy sun in a cloud-flecked sky. Though the weather was mild for the time of year, it was not too warm to take to the road for a marathon-length jog-trot.

At half-past nine Mr Carter backed the mini-bus out of the garage and drove on to the playground where most of the school were assembling to watch the final preparations and cheer the runners on their way. Under Matron's guidance the refreshments were checked and loaded, while Mr Wilkins stood by holding route maps and stop-watch with the running-schedule pinned to a clipboard.

Atkinson looked at the master in some surprise. "I didn't know you were coming too, sir."

"Of course I'm coming too. I'm the official referee, time-keeper, spare driver, if needed, and ambulance man all rolled into one."

"Ambulance!" Atkinson echoed. "It's not going to be dangerous, is it!"

Mr Wilkins smiled knowingly. "Blisters," he explained, producing a small first-aid box from his

The boys on the playground shouted their good wishes, and Jennings and Darbishire set off at a comfortable pace

pocket. "Bound to be some sore feet before the day's over, and a good thing, too." His smile grew broader. "If you've no blisters to show when you get back, those suspiciously-minded sponsors of yours may think you did the whole journey in the back of the bus."

As the hour approached, Jennings and Darbishire, the first pair of runners, took up their positions ahead of the bus while the rest of the team climbed into the back. Mr Carter was already in the driving seat waiting for the time-signal to come through on the car radio.

"Any moment now! Just waiting for the ten o'clock pips," he called through the window as a programme of light music came to an end. He turned up the volume control as the BBC interval jingle sounded, followed by the Greenwich time-signal denoting the hour.

Mr Carter pressed the car horn, the boys on the playground shouted their good wishes, and Jennings and Darbishire set off towards the school gates at a comfortable pace. The six-hour trek had begun.

The first part of the route led through Linbury village and on towards the market town of Dunhambury. At this early stage the runners were fresh, eager and buoyed up with excitement: Darbishire was able to keep abreast of his companion without too much effort. And when the first change-over was made at ten-thirty the boys were well ahead of schedule.

Venables and Temple who took over the baton for the second leg also forced the pace, and by the time Rumbelow and Atkinson had completed their first stint on the road the team had nearly twenty minutes running time in hand.

160

"You're going too fast," Mr Wilkins warned them when the mini-bus stopped for the change-over at half-past eleven. "So far you've only run once each. You'll be tired out before you get half way at this rate."

The runners took heed of the warning: they had lost much of their excitable, surplus energy and now they settled down to their jog-trotting resolutely.

There was a heavy shower of rain later in the morning and the boys trotted on wet, happy and determined. Skirting town centres, avoiding highways and keeping to minor roads, the runners jogged along at a steady pace: thirty minutes on foot followed by an hour in the van for rest and refreshment. Inside the vehicle the passengers spent the time badgering Mr Wilkins with questions about the schedule and plaguing his ears with the same terrible jokes he had heard so many times before.

Anyone less placid than Mr Carter would have found the driving conditions somewhat frustrating. For mile after mile he propelled the bus along winding lanes at an agonising snail's pace. Hugging the verge and scraping the hedges, he waved on streams of hooting drivers impatient to overtake, returning their black looks with an apologetic smile.

As the morning wore on, minor mishaps led to slight delays. Venables broke a shoe lace and valuable time was lost while Mr Wilkins replaced it with a piece of string. Rumbelow developed a blister and had to stop for first-aid treatment at the roadside, and Darbishire fell into a ditch while trying to avoid a shower of mud thrown up by a passing tractor.

At two o'clock, Mr Carter said, "Next pair stand by! I'll just get round the bend and we'll do the change-over."

Atkinson and Rumbelow struggled out of their sweaters and Darbishire asked the timekeeper, "How much further to go, sir?"

"Nine rough and hilly miles and barely two hours to do them in," said Mr Wilkins, consulting his clipboard. "If we get any more hold-ups we'll be in real trouble."

Once round the curve of the road a short blast on the car horn, told Temple and Venables that their stint was over. Gasping and blowing they returned to the van while the next pair took over the baton.

It was then that things started to go wrong, though at the time the trouble seemed trivial. Atkinson and Rumbelow, trotting forward round the next bend, found the road blocked by a herd of excited cows.

The boys stopped and turned to the van behind them for guidance. At once, Mr Wilkins poked his head out of the passenger window and shouted, "Run on, you boys! Never mind the cows: they won't hurt you."

"But there's nobody in charge of them: they've broken out," Rumbelow protested, pointing to the field beyond the hedge where a broken farm gate was swinging loosely on one hinge.

"You can get past them if you get down in the ditch."

"Yes, sir, but if—?"

"We'll look after the cows. You get on and run!"

Waving their arms and shouting, Atkinson and Rumbelow managed to clear a way through the far side of the herd. Meanwhile, the van came to a stop, hemmed in on all sides by prancing cows.

Darbishire stared through the windscreen in some trepidation. "Oh, fish-hooks, sir, whatever are we going to do?" he queried.

"*Do!* What d'you think we're going to do?" Mr Wilkins said impatiently. "Scream for help and hide under the seat?"

"No, not exactly, sir, but—"

"We're going to get them back in the field, that's what! Plenty of time to catch the runners up when we've done it."

So saying, Mr. Wilkins jumped down on to the roadway shouting, "Giddup, there! Giddup!" in the manner of a television cowboy. But instead of heading back towards the gateway the animals scattered widely up and down the lane. They seemed interested in the van: one of them pushed the wing mirror sideways with its nose while another scratched its horn along the paintwork of the sliding door.

"Everybody get out and help!" ordered the television cowboy. He waved his arms as though conducting the bovine choir gathered around him who were now moo-ing and bellowing with the full force of their lungs. The cows, though frisky, were not aggressive: indeed, they seemed puzzled by the shoo-ing and arm-waving antics of the boys who now came scrambling out of the van and went hopping about the lane, like fleas on a griddle. For a time all was chaos and confusion, but at last amidst much shouting, gesticulating and moo-ing the great cattle round-up got under way.

Meanwhile, safely removed from the hurly-burly of the jostling cows, Rumbelow and Atkinson trotted on, assuming that the van would catch up with them in a matter of minutes.

In this, they were disappointed; and, indeed, there was still no sign of the escort vehicle a quarter of an hour later when the lane they were following came out on to a slightly wider road which crossed their route at right angles.

Again the runners came to a halt. '*Now* which way?" panted Atkinson looking helplessly to left and right. "Old Wilkie never said anything about a T-junction."

"There ought to be a signpost," Rumbelow protested. "Why isn't there a signpost when we need one?"

"Well there isn't, so it's no good moaning. We'll just have to wait here till they catch us up."

Rumbelow flipped his fingers with frustration. "But we can't just hang around doing nothing. We'll be wasting our running time. Sir said we were behind schedule already."

They stared at each other uncertainly. Then they stared up and down the road, but there was no one about to help them solve their dilemma. Atkinson began to panic. "Come on! We've got to keep moving, whatever happens. We shan't get to Mrs Hockin's before dark – let alone four o'clock – if we stop here any longer."

"OK then – turn right," Rumbelow decided, setting off briskly on the route of his choice. "There's a good chance it's the right way, and even if it isn't—"

He broke off to save his breath for running, but Atkinson knew what he meant: with the four o'clock deadline drawing closer every minute, even a wrong decision seemed better than no decision at all.

It took the round-up party longer to drive the cows back into the field than Mr Wilkins had bargained for. To begin with, the boys were slow to realise that the best way to make a cow move in the required direction is to stand behind the animal and drive it forwards. Shouting orders at it to turn round, come back or wheel to the left was as useless as expecting the beast to mark time or stand to attention. Matters were further complicated by Darbishire who was given the job of opening and shutting the gate as occasion demanded. Unfortunately, when admitting one cow returning to the fold he would allow two or three more to escape again. By the time the whole herd was back in the field and the gate secured with a piece of string, Mr Wilkins was fuming with exasperation.

"Sir, please sir, how long before we catch up with Rumbelow and Atki," Jennings asked as Mr Carter started the van.

"They can't be all that far ahead. No need to panic," the master replied, letting in the clutch.

"I wasn't panicking, sir. It's just that it's time for Darbi and me to take over. The other two will be flaked out by now."

This was true enough, but Mr Carter wasn't worried as he expected to overtake the runners in the next half mile. Within minutes they were approaching the T-junction and Mr Wilkins called out, "Turn left at the corner."

Instead of turning, Mr Carter brought the van to a halt. "No signpost! How do we know which way the boys have gone?" he said.

Mr Wilkins frowned and tapped his clipboard. "The map says we go left," he insisted.

"Yes, of course. But Atkinson and Rumbelow didn't have a map. There's no sign of them: they could have gone either way."

By now it was well past the time for the change-over. Whichever way the runners had gone, they might well have run themselves to a standstill.

Mr Carter turned left at the junction and drove full speed up the hill. At the brow he stopped again, for the road ran straight as far as the eye could see. No sign of the runners! They couldn't possibly be so far ahead!

"Must have gone the other way. We'll have to go back and look for them," Mr Carter muttered as he turned the van in a gateway.

The boys in the back were growing uneasy. "We'll never do it in the time," Darbishire said, shaking his head gloomily. "All this messing about! If you ask me, it's goodbye to our seventy-two quid."

At twenty minutes to three Rumbelow stopped running.

"It's no good going on, Atki. It must be the wrong

way," he gasped out with what little breath he had left. "If they were coming, they'd have caught us up by now." His legs suddenly felt shaky and he flopped himself down on the bank by the roadside. "Anyway, I can't run any more."

His companion was only too willing to call a halt. They had been on the move for longer than they had expected and had now run out of steam.

"What are we going to do, then?" Atkinson demanded, panting heavily.

"Go back to that wrong turning and wait for the van."

"But they'll have gone past it by now, if they went the other way," Atkinson pointed out. Despair assailed him at the prospect of being stranded in unknown territory. "They may *never* find us – not till it's too late, anyway."

"Too late!" Rumbelow echoed in horror. "You mean we might die of exposure?"

"No, you clodpoll. I mean not till after four o'clock when the run's over. If we're not in Southcombe by then, we'll have had our chips."

Dispirited, Atkinson sank down on the bank beside his partner . . . But a moment later he was on his feet again, waving his arms and hopping from foot to foot in joyful relief. "Here they are!" he cried, as the mini-bus came speeding up the road towards them. "We're saved. Hooray! Hooray!"

No time was wasted in turning the van round and heading back the way they had come with the newly-found passengers aboard.

"Wow! Thought you'd gone without us, sir," Rumbelow said, subsiding on the back seat with a nervous giggle. "We didn't know which way to go at the junction, you see, and—"

"Save your breath, boy! We'll hear about it later," Mr Wilkins broke in. "We're nearly twenty minutes behind schedule, thanks to that wrong turning, and we've still got to get back to the junction before we can start running again." He consulted his list. "It's Jennings and Darbishire next. They'll have to get their skates on if we're going to make up all that lost time."

"Skates on, sir!" Jennings grinned and gave his running-partner a friendly punch in the ribs. "I don't know about you, Darbi, but I reckon muddy lanes are bad enough: I shouldn't want to do this lot on ice!"

At a quarter past three Jennings and Darbishire were recalled to the van as Mr Carter thought it best to cut down the running-time of each pair in an effort to speed up the over-all pace.

They were now four-and-a-half miles from Southcombe so, hastily revising the schedule, the masters decided that Venables and Temple must try to cover the next two miles in twenty minutes, and that this effort must be followed by a similar performance from Atkinson and Rumbelow. Then, with half a mile to cover and five minutes to do it in, Jennings and Darbishire would summon up their last ounce of stamina for the final lap.

That was the plan – in theory! In practice, it didn't work out like that at all.

Venables and Temple had been sent on ahead while

Mr Carter and Mr Wilkins were revising the time-table, and they were out of sight and running well when Mr Carter switched on the engine and pressed the self-starter.

The engine failed to respond! Frowning, he tried again – with the same result. After some half a dozen unsuccessful attempts, he shook his head slowly and said, "Sorry, lads, we're in real trouble now."

The boys in the back were aghast at this latest development. "But what is it, sir? What's the matter?" they cried.

Mr Carter – and Mr Wilkins, too – knew only too well what the trouble was. The school mini-bus, though normally a most reliable vehicle, had an infuriating habit of developing trouble in its petrol pump at inconvenient moments. It didn't happen often, and when it did the matter could always be put right: after which, the engine would behave perfectly – until the next time!

"Can you mend it, sir?" Darbishire asked anxiously.

"Given the time, I can," Mr Carter replied. "The trouble is it might take ten minutes – or it might take half an hour."

"Half an hour!" The boys in the back gasped in horror. "But that means we shan't be able to relieve Venables and Temple."

"It could mean that," Mr Carter agreed, fiddling through the tool box behind the driver's seat. He selected a screwdriver and a pair of pliers. "Come on, Wilkins, give me a hand. The sooner we get the petrol pump off, the better."

Without wasting a moment, the masters jumped

down from the van, opened the bonnet and set to work on the faulty pump. But everyone knew in his heart that it was useless. With every second ticking away the team's chance of success, even a short delay would prove fatal.

Rumbelow flicked his fingers in despair, "We can't wait while they do it. Not even ten minutes – let alone half an hour. Temple and Ven will conk out if we're not there to take over."

"What can we do?" moaned Darbishire.

Jennings jumped to his feet. "There's only one thing for it. We'll have to hitch a lift," he said.

They looked at him without hope. "Fat chance we've got out here in these lanes," said Atkinson. "We haven't seen more than a dozen cars since we left the main road."

Jennings was looking out of the rear window. "There's one coming now," he said.

They swung round to look for themselves.

"I can't see a car," said Rumbelow.

"Not now, you can't. Wait till it comes round the bend. I just caught sight of it coming over the top of the hill."

Hope glimmered once more. "What shall we do, Jen? Shall we flag it?"

"We can try," Jennings said excitedly. "We'll all try. Quick, everybody, out on the road! It's our only chance."

Within seconds the boys were out of the van and ranged up, two on each side of the road. They waited, tense and expectant, staring at the empty road behind the van. Then, in the distance, they saw a large white car coming towards them, travelling fast.

"It won't stop. I bet it won't stop," Darbishire muttered. He crossed his fingers and made a bargain with Fate. "Make it stop! Please let it stop and I'll promise to work harder in class and never forget my music practice."

The bargain with Fate hung in the balance for some seconds as the car sped towards them and the boys jumped up and down waving handkerchiefs and sweaters. At first it appeared that the driver had no intention of stopping, for the car was travelling at speed – too fast, in fact, to overtake the stationary mini-bus in safety.

"It's slowing down! It'll *have* to slow down," Atkinson shouted in high glee, slithering down the bank on to the roadway with reckless bravado.

They all yelled at him. "Get back, Atki! Get out of the road – you'll get run over!"

He jumped for safety with only seconds to spare. The car slowed to pass the van, then accelerated again while the boys' spirits dropped to absolute zero.

Then, unexpectedly, the car pulled into the nearside verge and stopped some fifty yards further on.

Chapter 14

Journey's End

The first thing they noticed as they raced towards the mud-splashed car drawn up at the roadside was that the driver, a dark-haired woman in her forties, looked extremely annoyed at being commanded to stop in such a peremptory fashion. She wound down the window and said, "Well, what is it?"

Her tone was not inviting, but the situation was desperate, so Jennings said, "I'm awfully sorry, but something terrible has happened. We're on a sponsored run, you see, and we've got to get to Southcombe by four o'clock, and our van's broken down."

"Sponsored run!" she echoed. "Well, I may be a bit slow in the uptake, but if you're supposed to be doing it on foot, what on earth do you need a van for?"

"It's a relay," he explained. "Two of the runners have gone on ahead, and we've got to relieve them in a quarter of an hour or we'll never do it."

"I see." There was a pause while the driver considered the information. Then, unexpectedly, she dropped her forbidding expression and laughed. "Well, that seems clear enough," she said. "What are we waiting for? You'd all better get in."

The boys almost fell over themselves in expressing their gratitude. In fact, Darbishire *did* fall over his feet in doing a Dervish dance of appreciation and landed in a puddle in the middle of the road.

"This is marvellous! Ever so kind of you! We'd never do it, otherwise," Atkinson sang out as he climbed into the back of the car.

It occurred to Jennings that Mr Carter and Mr Wilkins ought to be informed of the latest development. With a brief "Excuse me a minute" to the woman at the wheel, he rushed back to the mini-van where the masters were still in the process of dismantling the petrol pump. Indeed, they had been so engrossed in their repair work that they had barely noticed what was happening fifty yards along the road.

"Sir, sir, we've been offered a lift," Jennings shouted as he skidded to a halt beside the van. "A lady's offered to take us to catch up with Venables and Temple."

Mr Carter looked up from the depths of the engine. "I shall need to know a bit more about who you're going with," he said. "You can't just accept lifts from people you don't know."

"Oh, but she's ever so nice, sir, and it's our only chance of getting to Southcombe on time," Jennings pleaded. 'If you'd just come and meet her, sir, I'm sure you'd say it was all right."

Mr Carter wiped his oily hands on a piece of rag. "Lead the way, then. I'll come and have a word with her," he agreed.

Leaving his colleague to carry on the repairs to the faulty petrol pump, Mr Carter followed Jennings back to the white car.

"Fair enough! You can't be too careful," the driver agreed when Mr Carter explained the school rule about hitch-hiking. She fumbled in the depths of her hand-bag, produced her driving licence and passed it out through the window.

"There you are!" she went on. "Now you know my name and address." She laughed. "It even tells you how old I am."

Mr Carter smiled as he returned the driving licence. "Very well, then! Permission granted," he called to the squashed occupants of the rear seats. As Jennings joined them and the car moved forward, he added, "We'll see you at Southcombe when we've got the petrol pump sorted out."

"Right-ho, sir. Goodbye!"

"Oh, and another thing! Get Mrs Hockin to check the exact time of your arrival. That's most important".

It seemed no time at all before the passengers in the mud-splashed white car spotted Venables and Temple trotting along on the road ahead. By this time the boys had learned that their driver's name was Mrs Seymour, and that they would not be taking her out of her way as she was, in any case, bound for Southcombe. She had not, of course, intended to travel the later stages of the journey at a mere five miles an hour; but having heard all about their project she sportingly agreed to follow the runners and take over the duties of an escort driver.

They pulled up on overtaking Venables and Temple and explained the changed situation. At 3.35 pm they stopped again: Venables and Temple got into the car and Rumbelow and Atkinson started their final run.

It was shortly after this that Mrs Seymour said, "I don't want to be a wet blanket, boys, but if your deadline is four o'clock, I don't think you're going to do it."

Jennings refused to be daunted. The last signpost had read "Southcombe 2 miles".

"There's Darbishire and me to run yet," he pointed out. "We're holding ourselves ready to do a sprint in the last five minutes."

Mrs Seymour shook her head doubtfully. "From what I remember of the road it's a fair step from here to this place called *The Retreat*."

They were in Southcombe now, passing the railway station; and for the first time that day Jennings recognised a familiar landmark. They were following the road that he and Emma had taken when they had brought Ben and the other pets to Mrs Hockin's.

It was five minutes to four. By the road it was at least a mile to *The Retreat* – and he and Darbishire were no five-minute milers.

Then he remembered the short cut across Major Rudkin's land. If they took that route they still had a chance. Even as he weighed up the odds, the overgrown stile came into view a hundred yards ahead.

"We'll take the short cut," he said, and turned to Mrs Seymour. "Will you give the runners a honk. Slight change of plan! We're going another way."

175

Rumbelow and Atkinson were quick to see the advantage. "We'll come with you," Atkinson said, panting heavily. "We can keep going. We'll do the last lap together."

"OK, then! Get moving!"

"Including us!" Venables sang out, pushing Temple out on to the road.

Moments later all six boys were scrambling over the wired-up stile that marked the entrance to Major Rudkin's land.

Mrs Seymour watched from the car and shrugged off their excited cries of thanks and farewell.

"Don't waste your breath on me, boys," she called back. "And it's not goodbye. I'm coming round by the road: I want to know what happens. See you there!"

Heedless of the barbed wire, the boys scrambled through the barrier and set of along the right-of-way. It was close on four o'clock. There wasn't a second to lose.

Jennings led the way with the others close on his heels. They had gone a hundred yards when a gunshot rang out away to their left.

Darbishire panicked. "Get down everybody! Lie flat! It's old Major Trigger-Happy," he squawked.

"It's all right," Jennings shouted, still running strongly. "It's a public footpath. He can't stop us."

"He can if he's got a gun," said Temple. "He's shooting at us."

"He's not. He wouldn't dare. He's only trying to frighten us off. Come on, everybody – this way."

In the middle distance an enraged voice was

shouting, "Hey there! You! Stop, will you! Come here, I say! Stop, will you!"

The boys took no notice. With Jennings in the lead they pressed on along the overgrown pathway towards *The Retreat* while the Major's threats faded into the distance.

Soon they were over the boundary. On the far side of the paddock they could see Mrs Hockin feeding the goats. They rushed towards her shouting their greetings.

She looked up, surprised. "Well, well! Hullo, boys! How nice to see you," she said. There was a lack of urgency in her voice which drenched the boys' excitement like a douche of cold water.

"It's the sponsored run! We've arrived," Jennings shouted.

"It's the *what* dear?"

"The sponsored run. Aren't you expecting us?"

Mrs Hockin searched her memory. "Oh yes, of course. I remember now. Your master rang up and told me. I'd completely forgotten you were coming." She tut-tutted in self-reproach. "My fault entirely. My late husband always said I'd got a memory like a sieve. Did you have a nice journey?"

Nice journey! They were in a state of collapse, breathless and sagging at the knees with exhaustion. Even so, Jennings remembered the essential question.

"The time!" he cried. "What time is it?"

Mrs Hockin looked vague. "The time, dear?" she echoed, surprised that anyone should sound so concerned about such an unimportant matter. She looked at her watch. "Well, my watch says twenty past eleven, but it's said that for weeks."

"We must find out – it's vital."

None of the runners was wearing a wristwatch, so in desperation Jennings dashed past his hostess and into the house.

The kitchen clock had stopped at ten minutes to nine on some unspecified day in the past. Jennings ran into the living room where a transistor radio was playing chamber music. There was no clock, and as he looked about him wondering where to try next, the radio music came to an end. There followed the BBC interval jingle, and the familiar pips of the Greenwich time signal.

Four o'clock . . . They had done it!

Jennings turned to rush back into the garden, only to find that the rest of the team – and Mrs Hockin too – had followed him into the house just as the four o'clock time check came on to the air.

Wild rejoicing took place: muddy running shoes danced with abandon all over the carpet: cheers of triumph disturbed the cats snoozing on the stable window sills outside.

"We've done it! We've done it! Right on the dot! Fantastic."

"Success! Success!"

"Phew! Hold me up! I can't believe it."

Mrs Hockin hurried to make amends for her forget-fulness. Within ten minutes of the boys' arrival, she had brewed an enormous pot of tea for the thirsty runners and was busy frying bacon and eggs to assuage appetites that had had to make do with fruit juice and lumps of cheese since setting out on their journey.

While they ate, they told her about the day's adventures. She listened attentively and seemed deeply impressed by all the arrangements they had had to make.

"I'd no idea it had to be planned like a time-table; but then, I don't know much about sponsored runs and that sort of thing." she said as she poured out still more cups of tea.

"Ah, but it was absolutely worth it," Jennings told her. "You see, we'll be able to collect £72 from the people who promised to back us. And I had a letter from Emma the day before yesterday," he went on eagerly. "She says she'd found enough people to sponsor our team for the same amount. So if you add all that together, plus what we made at the Animal Fair we'll have raised over £200. Not bad, eh!"

It was clear that Mrs Hockin was deeply moved by the boys' efforts to help, but at the same time she looked very worried. Finally, she said in a low voice, "So very, very kind of you! All this trouble you've taken! All the work you've done!"

"And the money, Mrs Hockin – the two-hundred-and-whatever-it-is pounds," Jennings went on. "Will it be enough to buy your new fences?"

She smiled and said, "Never mind about that. We won't go into it now."

"No, but will it?" he persisted. After all, they had a right to know!

This time she sighed sadly and replied, "Frankly, no,

I'm afraid. You see, this stock-proof fencing I've got to put up works out at the ridiculous figure of £10 a foot."

They stared at her in disbelief. "A *foot*!" Darbishire echoed. He struggled briefly with a problem in mental arithmetic. "But that means that all the money we've raised will only buy about twenty feet of fence – if that!"

She nodded. "That's all, I'm afraid. About the length of this room."

"And how many feet will you need altogether?" Venables asked.

"Getting on for a thousand, I believe, if it's to go all round the boundary."

There was a stunned silence round the tea-table. Even Temple stopped eating.

"Twenty feet out of a thousand! Just a drop in the ocean – a mere flea-bite," Atkinson said bitterly.

"Don't worry, my dears," Mrs Hockin consoled them. "You can't do any more about it. You've done enough as it is."

"Yes, but all the same!" Jennings clicked his teeth in frustration. "£10 a *foot* and we've run all the way here from Linbury at five pence a *mile*! It just doesn't make sense."

Through the open window they heard the sound of a car approaching. Rumbelow looked out expecting to see the mini-bus: but it was Mrs Seymour in the mud-splashed estate car.

"I got delayed in the village, but I felt I must come

and find out what happened," she said when the boys went out to greet her. "Did you get here in time?"

"Yes, but only just," Jennings replied. He introduced her to Mrs Hockin who had already heard during tea of the vital part Mrs Seymour had played on the last stage of the run.

"I was coming this way, in any case," the newcomer explained as she was ushered into the house for a cup of tea. "Southcombe is on my list, you see."

"Your list?" Mrs Hockin looked puzzled.

"My house-hunting list. Well, it's not so much house-hunting as stable-hunting. What with landlords and property-developers breathing down my neck, I've got to find a new home for my horses."

It appeared that Mrs Seymour had, for some years, been running a riding stables at a village about ten miles from Southcombe. Now, however, her lease of the premises was about to expire and her landlord was unwilling to renew it. "So if I don't find somewhere soon, my horses and I will be out on the street," she said with a rueful laugh.

Mrs Hockin knew all about the problems involved where livestock was concerned "People just don't realise that animals have needs as well as human beings," she said with a touch of righteous indignation in her voice. "I have terrible battles with my neighbour over my little menagerie."

"So I understand. The boys told me about your sanctuary as we came along in the car."

Mrs Hockin smiled modestly. "It sounds rather grand calling it a sanctuary," she said. "It's more like a permanent camp-site for four-footed geriatrics. Dogs, cats, goats, donkeys. You name it – we feed it! Perhaps you'd like to have a look round."

There was still an hour of daylight left as Mrs Hockin led her visitors out of doors to say hello to the animals. And though the runners were leg-weary, none of them chose to stay behind.

Jennings, in particular, was overjoyed at the chance of renewing acquaintance with Emma's secret menagerie: there were so many things he must remember to tell her when he again got round to writing her a letter.

Ben, for instance, had grown enormously since July, but was still as excitable and puppy-like as ever. The large white rabbit contentedly nibbling a carrot looked a very different animal from the miserable specimen they had rescued from that terrible pet shop. And there were the gerbils, as lively as ever. Jennings laughed to himself at the memory of poor old Mrs – er – er (he couldn't remember her name). Anyway, the one who'd shouted, "Rats at the window, trying to get in!" He hadn't meant to upset the good ladies: it was just the way things had turned out. It was the same with the hedgehog he'd hidden under the tea-towel. *T't!* That had caused as much panic as though it had been a man-eating tiger.

He turned to Mrs Hockin and asked, "Have you still got our hedgehog?"

"He's about somewhere," she replied. "He's a bit of a loner, you know. Just turns up for a snack when he feels like it. We don't see a great deal of him."

Jennings was overjoyed at the chance of renewing acquaintance with Emma's secret menagerie

"You're lucky to have this place," said Mrs Seymour who had been appraising the stables with a professional air. "I wish I could find somewhere like it for my horses."

Her hostess nodded sympathetically. "I hope you do. It's not easy finding anywhere to rent these days. And then there's the upkeep, of course." She shrugged and made a little despairing gesture. "We're both in the same boat, really. If I don't soon find the money to replace all my tumbledown fences, I'll be out on my ear too – like you and your horses."

Just then, Mr Carter and Mr Wilkins arrived in the mini-bus. The petrol-pump had been unco-operative and the repair had taken them a great deal of time.

The boys swarmed round the masters proclaiming their success at the tops of their voices. "We did it, sir! We got here just in time! Isn't that terrific."

Mrs Hockin greeted Mr Carter as an old friend, then turned to Mr Wilkins. "How d'you do! I understand you're the cook," she said.

Mr Wilkins was nonplussed. "Cook!" he echoed. "I'm not a cook. I'm a schoolmaster."

"But weren't you in charge of the catering at the summer camp?"

"Oh, I see what you mean," Mr Wilkins replied, simmering down.

"Yes, indeed. I clearly remember the boys telling me what wonderful meals you were providing for them in camp."

The six culprits turned away trying to stifle their laughter. But Mr Wilkins shrugged off the doubtful compliment with a modest smile. "We did our best," he said with dignity.

After that it was time to go, for Mr Carter was hoping to be back in Linbury in time for school supper. The boys said goodbye, climbed aboard and sank down wearily in the back of the van.

As they drove away, Jennings waved and went on waving through the rear window. Mrs Hockin was holding Ben in her arms, manipulating one fore-paw to make him wave back.

The mini-bus turned the corner and Mrs Hockin put the dog down on the cobblestones. "So kind of them, don't you think, Mrs Seymour," she observed, turning back towards the stables. "All that hard work they've put in, just for me and my fences. I can't possibly take their money, of course. It wouldn't be right. After all, it's not as though I was a registered charity or anything like that."

It is doubtful whether Mrs Seymour heard her. She was standing in the entrance to the stables looking around her intently. At last, she said, "I've got an idea, Mrs Hockin. It may be a non-starter, but I think it's worth discussing. Shall we go back into the house?"

Chapter 15

Last Night of Term

It was some weeks later that Jennings received a letter from Mrs Hockin. She had previously written to Mr Carter thanking the team for their efforts on the sponsored run; and now it seemed she had a special announcement which she was sure the boys would like to hear.

The letter said, "Such splendid news! And if it hadn't been for your mini-bus breaking down, it would never have happened."

Jennings was reading the letter aloud at the breakfast table. At this point he cast his eye down the page, reading silently – to the exasperation of those seated around him.

"Well, go on," urged Temple, seething with curiosity. "Tell us what *has* happened."

"Oh, sorry. I forgot you were listening." Jennings turned back to the first paragraph. "You will be pleased to hear that Mrs Seymour and I are joining forces and she will shortly be moving into *The Retreat* – plus her horses, of course. It seemed the obvious answer with all my empty stables going begging.

"The splendid thing is, of course, that it has solved the financial crisis at a stroke," the letter went on. "With a flourishing riding school on the premises we can afford to replace those fences that Major Rudkin has been so tiresome about, so I suggest we donate the money that you boys and Emma have raised to some worthwhile charity concerned with animal welfare."

The suggestion gave rise to some argument round the breakfast table, but on the whole the boys were in favour of the arrangement. They were in favour, too, of Mrs Hockin's invitation to all concerned to pay another visit to *The Retreat* during the Christmas holidays to see for themselves how well a ramshackle animal sanctuary and a businesslike riding stables could carry on side by side.

Emma Sparrow also had a letter from Mrs Hockin, couched in similar terms. But the final paragraph was different. It read:

"My partner, Mrs Seymour and I will be taking the horse-box to Hertfordshire on Wednesday week, to collect a colt. We shall be returning home through your part of London, so I thought we'd call to let you know how your animals are getting on, and perhaps stay for a cup of tea. Let me know if this would suit you."

Emma let her know! And on the following Wednesday week Mrs Sparrow held a tea-party at 72 Gaitskell Court. Angela Birkinshaw was there and, needless to say, so were Emma, Maggie and Cleo, who made sure of getting back from school in good time to welcome the visitors from Southcombe.

Everybody had to be introduced to somebody, for

none of those present had met all the other members of the group. But that didn't matter – there was plenty to talk about. From Jane Seymour the girls heard about the final stage of the sponsored run; from Mrs Hockin they learned how *The Retreat* with its stables and paddock was being adapted as a riding school without disturbing the animals already in residence.

"Where's the new colt?" Emma demanded, almost before tea was over. "May we see him?"

Mrs Seymour nodded. "He's in the horsebox behind the car. That reminds me," she went on, rising to her feet. "I must let him out of the trailer to stretch his legs before we go."

Her partner looked alarmed. "What – *here*?" she cried in some concern. "My dear woman, you can't exercise horses in Brixton Road. It's jam-packed solid with traffic."

Jane Seymour shrugged. "I'll have to do *something*."

"He could stretch his legs outside in the courtyard," Aunt Angela suggested. "Plenty of room and no traffic."

"Yes, why not?" Emma cried excitedly. "May we walk him for you, Mrs Seymour? We'll be ever so careful."

There was no reason to decline their offer. "Come along, then, you girls. Just a quickie round the block," Mrs Seymour agreed. "I'll come down and introduce you to him."

Mr Fagg was up on the fourth floor changing a light

bulb outside the lift when the sound of strident female voices came billowing along the corridor towards him.

"Disgraceful! Shouldn't ought to be allowed," squawked the first voice. "Out there on the courtyard as bold as brass, for everyone to see."

"Best go and complain right away," said the second strident voice. "Make sure that caretaker does his duty properly, this time!"

The caretaker in question groaned inwardly and stuffed his duster into his overall pocket. Here he was trapped on top of a step-ladder with no means of escape, and Mrs Pratt and Mrs Plumrose closing in on him, getting ready to pounce.

A moment later they spied the step-ladder and he was in their clutches.

"Mr Fagg! Just the person we want," Mrs Pratt began. "It's disgraceful. It's not often I complain, but—"

"No, no, of course not," he assured her, coming down from his ladder.

"It's that Emma Sparrow up in Flat 72! No business to be keeping dangerous animals on the premises."

"And it's not the first time, either," Mrs Plumrose added. "All those creatures prowling about loose last summer. It was us who told you about them, wasn't it!"

Mr Fagg dutifully cast his mind back to the previous July. "I remember! Flying rats dangling in space outside the window! And wasn't there a man-eating hedgehog disguised as a pin-cushion, as well?" He drew in his breath in mock horror and gave a little shudder.

"But that's all old history as you might say," he went on. "Emma Sparrow hasn't got any animals now."

Mrs Plumrose smirked in triumph. "She *has*, you know! And not just little animals this time. *She's got a horse!*"

It was as well that Mr Fagg had already descended from the step-ladder, for he fell about laughing in a way that would have been dangerous if he had not had his feet on the ground. So Emma Sparrow kept a horse in Flat 72, did she! How did she get it there? he inquired. Ride it up the stairs, or run it up in the lift? He was about to add that it was not April Fools' Day when Mrs Pratt broke in angrily, "You've no call to make a joke of it, Mr Fagg. Just go down to the court-yard and see for yourself. That'll make you eat your words!"

He was puzzled by the tone of conviction in the women's voices. They weren't joking! They actually *believed* this incredible story!

"All right, ladies, I'm on my way," he said, pressing the button for the lift. "Anything for a quiet life."

As the lift shot down to the ground floor, Mrs Pratt frowned and shook her head.

"I don't know what things are coming to – really I don't," she grumbled. "We never had this sort of carry-on in the old days – horses and all that!"

Her neighbour gave the matter some thought. "Well, not lately perhaps, but we did used to," she replied. "We always had horses when I was a girl."

"*You* did! *You* had horses!" Mrs Pratt was

astounded. Somehow she couldn't picture the portly Mrs Plumrose on horseback.

"No, not me, myself. I didn't have a horse. I'm talking about the milkman. Used to come up our street with a horse and cart regular every morning when I was a girl."

Mrs Pratt sniffed and said, "This one Emma Sparrow's got isn't a milkman's horse. It isn't even pulling a milk float. T't! I don't know what things are coming to!"

"No more do I. T't, t't! t't!"

They stood tut-tutting together as they waited for the lift to come up so they could go down and start spreading the news of the scandalous goings-on of Emma Sparrow on every landing throughout the block.

It was a beautiful colt: the girls were agreed about that, even though none of them could claim to be much of a horsewoman. Mrs Seymour released the colt from the trailer and the girls took it in turns to hold the bridle as the animal was led round the courtyard. There was, of course, no chance of allowing it to run free in such surroundings, but, even so, it appeared to be happy enough trotting round the courtyard with its three devoted escorts.

After ten minutes of the colt's trotting, walking, restrained prancing, head-tossing and pawing the tarmac, the girls were on the point of taking the animal back to the horse-box where Mrs Seymour was waiting. They stopped, however, as a cry of indignation rang out from the steps of the main entrance on the far side of the courtyard. "Hey! You girls, there! Emma! Cleo!" the voice roared.

"Stand by for trouble," Emma warned her companions. "Mr Fagg doesn't sound too pleased."

The girls looked at one another and grinned. With a conspiratorial wink, Emma added, "I think we might pull his leg, though. Just very gently, of course."

Moments later, Mr Fagg had made his way across the courtyard. "Cor! Stone the crows! You girls will get me the sack," he expostulated. "I had enough of you and your perishing animals last time. Get this one off the premises at once before anyone else sees it."

"Oh, but you can't mean that, Mr Fagg," said Maggie, wide-eyed with innocence. "He's come to stay. After all he won't be any trouble – just a dear little stray pony who followed us home and won't go away."

"We could easily make him a stable out of that spare dustbin shed of yours," Cleo suggested, beaming her broadest smile at the outraged caretaker.

To begin with, Mr Fagg didn't seem to realise that they were pulling his leg, or, if he *did* realise it, he couldn't see anything to laugh at.

"Now, look here, you lot," he rumbled in his deep, gravelly voice, "I've stood up for you girls in the past – and that hasn't always been easy, what with old Mother Plumrose and all breathing down my neck." He paused and glowered at the chief culprit. "But this time, young Emma, you've gone too far. What's the housing manager going to say when he's told you've been turning the courtyard into a circus with a prancing great horse charging round the blocks?"

Emma looked contrite. Perhaps the joke had mis-fired. "Only fooling, Mr Fagg!" she said humbly.

"Eh?"

"This pony's not staying here. He's on his way to a riding-stables at Southcombe."

"Oh! . . . Oh, I see! . . . That's different, then!"

"Yes, and we're going too, after Christmas," Maggie told him. "We've been invited to go and lend a hand with the animals before we go back to school. How about that, then!"

Mr Fagg gave a little grunt and said, "Best news I've heard for a long time. The sooner I see the back of you lot, the better."

Maggie was shocked at his tone of voice. "You needn't say it like that, Mr Fagg. I thought, perhaps, you'd miss us when we'd gone."

"Huh! Not on your nelly! It'll be a real old rest cure without you girls around, making trouble all day."

It was the girls' turn to be taken in. They hadn't thought he'd felt like that about them! The little joke didn't seem funny any more.

Emma shrugged, gave a jerk to the bridle and started leading the colt back to the horse-box. "Sorry we've caused you so much trouble, Mr Fagg," she called back over her shoulder.

They were halfway across the courtyard when they heard him calling after them. "Emma! Cleo! Maggie! Just a minute!"

He didn't actually *run* to catch up with them, but he hurried his pace to show that he wasn't going to let them get away before he'd had the final word.

"It's just this," he said slowing to a stop beside them. "This invitation you've got for the Christmas holidays. Don't stay away too long, that's all. This is your home, don't forget."

For a man of his brusque manner he sounded absurdly diffident. Maggie said, "I thought you wanted to get rid of us. You said something about having a nice quiet time without us making trouble for you all over the place."

Mr Fagg pursed his lips and scratched his scrubby blue chin. "Maybe I did, but you can have a bit too much peace and quiet," he admitted. "Shan't know myself without you girls cluttering the place up, so – as I was saying – don't stay away too long. Besides—"

He stopped short, looking rather sheepish. He hadn't meant to let his feelings show. A grudging tolerance of the girls was as much as he was willing to admit to, in public. He fumbled for his handkerchief to cover his embarrassment but, in his confusion, he blew his nose on his duster by mistake. "T't! You girls will get me the sack!" he said as he turned back towards the flats. "You're more worry to me than all my money!"

The girls looked at one another and grinned. Good old Mr Fagg! He might *look* like a wet blanket, he might *sound* like a moaning fog-horn, but his heart was in the right place – and that's what really mattered!

It was the last night of the Christmas term. Once again the corridors landings and dormitories of Linbury Court School had echoed to the sound of *Crossing off the Days*, bellowed in unison by seventy-nine penetrating treble voices.

Mr Carter, the duty master, strolled round the building keeping a watchful eye on the end-of-term-celebrations. He was accompanied by Mr Wilkins who, having at last finished his termly reports, was feeling cheerful at the prospect of four weeks' holiday ahead. When they reached Dormitory Four, the song was over and the singers, tired and excited, were going through the motions of getting ready to go to sleep.

In the bed at the far end, Jennings sat propped against his pillow talking into his tooth-mug microphone.

"Chief Game Warden calling HQ," he was saying. "I am now heading North over Wildlife Reserve at two thousand feet. Drought conditions down below look serious. There's a herd of wildebeeste stampeding across the plain looking for water. Stand by while I try and chivvy them towards the drinking-hole."

The Chief Game Warden ceased broadcasting as the masters came to a stop at the foot of his bed.

"What's this nonsense about stampeding wildebeeste making for the drinking hole?" Mr Wilkins demanded jovially. "It sounds to me like Form Three lining up for cocoa."

Mr Carter laughed. "It's a welcome change from those moon exploration activities that we had to put up with at the end of last term."

Jennings agreed with Mr Carter. "Space travel's a bit old hat at the moment, sir," he admitted. "That's why Darbishire and I have gone over to wildlife

195

conservation instead. It's something you can actually *do*, instead of just playing at it."

His friend nodded confirmation from the bed across the gangway. "We just can't wait till we get to Mrs Hockin's after Christmas, sir, so we can get stuck into it."

Mr Carter was puzzled. It was the first he'd heard of another visit to Southcombe.

"Yes, didn't you know, sir?" Darbishire went on. "Jennings had a letter from her weeks ago: she wants all the blokes on the sponsored run to spend a couple of days at *The Retreat* before we come back to school next term."

"And not only us, but there's a girl called Emma Sparrow and her friends as well," said Jennings.

Mr Carter nodded. He had heard a lot about Emma when Aunt Angela had telephoned him about the sponsored run.

"Yes, well, we're all going to make it a special animal conservation visit," Jennings explained. "It'll be hard work, too, because as well as looking after Mrs Hockin's animals we're going to help get the stables ready for the riding school."

Mr Wilkins had been listening to the explanation with the indulgent expression that is often seen on the faces of staff when the hard work of the term is over. Suddenly, he clapped his hand to his brow and cried, "This is terrible! Mrs Hockin must be warned! The horses must be warned! Goats, donkeys – anything on four legs must be told of the fate that awaits them."

Dormitory Four sat upright in their beds exchanging

knowing winks and delighted glances. Old Wilkie must be in a super-fantastic, end-of-term mood to lay on a bogus pantomime for their benefit.

"Why, sir? Why?" they cried, egging him on.

"It's obvious!" Mr Wilkins boomed at them, pacing the dormitory with long strides and waving his arms in dramatic gestures. "Here is this old-world, peaceful, animal sanctuary! Just picture it – elderly horses snoozing in the sun, doddering donkeys dozing on doorsteps, antiquated goats grazing on garbage dumps – in short, a haven of repose for harmless beasts!"

He paused, while they pictured it; then, waving his arms in even wilder circles he cried, "And now see what is about to happen! Jennings, Darbishire, Venables and others – to say nothing of a gaggle of excitable females – are about to descend upon this quiet rural backwater, destroying the peace, shattering the serenity and sending the animals running for cover in all directions."

"Oh *sir*!" protested Dormitory Four, rocking in their beds with delight. Old Wilkie was excelling himself! It was amazing how the prospect of four weeks' holiday mellowed the mood of hard-hearted schoolmasters!

"Poor Mrs Hockin! Poor old horses!" The master's voice trembled with bogus sympathy. "Little does the poor woman know what horrors await her with the arrival of Jennings and his band of helpers."

Jennings grinned like a toothpaste advertisement. "She'll know soon enough when we get there, sir," he said cheerfully. "We'll tell you all about it when we get back next term."

"*Next term!*" Mr Wilkins uttered a hollow groan. "Don't remind me! Somehow or other, Mr Carter and I have managed to stagger along to the end of this term without cracking under the strain. But who can tell what terrors next term may hold in store!"

So saying, he tottered limply out of the dormitory to the accompaniment of cheers from his audience in the beds flanking the gangway. Mr Wilkins' self-mocking melodrama of the long-suffering teacher always went down well with the boys, but it was only on rare occasions, such as the last night of term, that he was willing to let himself go without restraint.

Mr Carter said, "Goodnight," switched off the light and followed his colleague out of the dormitory.

As the sound of the masters' footsteps died away along the landing, Jennings said, "It's all very well old Sir *pretending* next term scares him rigid, but I bet he's looking forward to it, on the quiet."

"Think so?" queried Darbishire, settling down in bed.

"Well, of course! He's got no one to boss around in the holidays, but as soon as he gets back here next term, he'll soon find something to moan about."

"Such as *what*?" Darbishire demanded.

It was dark in the dormitory, but Jennings hurled a pillow in the general direction of his friend's bed. Typical of old Darbi to ask silly questions!

"How do *I* know what's going to happen next term!" said Jennings. "There's Christmas and Mrs Hockin's to think about first. And after that—" He paused wrinkling his nose in thought. "Well, after that we'll be back here again. We'll just have to wait and see what happens, shan't we?"

All Pan Books are available at your local bookshop or newsagent, or can be ordered direct from the publisher. Indicate the number of copies required and fill in the form below.

Send to: Pan C. S. Dept
                Macmillan Distribution Ltd
                Houndmills Basingstoke RG21 2XS
or phone: 0256 29242, quoting title, author and Credit Card number.

Please enclose a remittance* to the value of the cover price plus £1.00 for the first book plus 50p per copy for each additional book ordered.

*Payment may be made in sterling by UK personal cheque, postal order, sterling draft or international money order, made payable to Pan Books Ltd.

Alternatively by Barclaycard/Access/Amex/Diners

Card No.

Expiry Date

Signature

Applicable only in the UK and BFPO addresses.

While every effort is made to keep prices low, it is sometimes necessary to increase prices at short notice. Pan Books reserve the right to show on covers and charge new retail prices which may differ from those advertised in the text or elsewhere.

NAME AND ADDRESS IN BLOCK LETTERS PLEASE

....

Name _____

Address_____

_____

_____

_____

3/87